Sufficient Evidence

A Novel
By Al Macy
AlMacyAuthor.com

Chapter One

DEAN SHIPLEY THOUGHT HE was alone in the forest. His workers had gone home, and he sat on a redwood stump, admiring his cannabis crop. Taking off his cap, he wiped his forehead and brushed his long hair away from his neck. The sun had set an hour earlier, but the temperature was still in the nineties. The raspy calls of cicadas surrounded him, and the skunky odor from his plants filled the air. *The smell of success.* This would be his last illegal grow. Two months to go, and his years as an outlaw would be over.

The crack of a shotgun shell made Dean jump. He stood and spun around. *A tripwire was triggered!* He scanned the woods, straining to see what might have set it off. His plants weren't mature enough to invite thieves. *Probably a raccoon or a bear. Maybe a mountain lion.* His hand went to his gun, but it wasn't in his pocket. He'd left it in the cabin. All the growers carried guns. His area of Humboldt County, known as Murder Mountain, had much more crime than outsiders realized.

He caught a flash of movement too far above the ground to be anything but a bear or a man. Dean cut his reflection time short and ran down the trail toward his cabin.

The first bullet entered four inches below his right shoulder. It blasted through the scapula, glanced off a rib, and exited from the center of his chest.

The second bullet penetrated the back of his neck. It burned through muscle tissue and the carotid artery before exiting below his chin.

The third bullet grazed a tree trunk before hitting him. It burst through the right side of his skull above the ear and, like a motorcycle in a steel mesh globe at a circus, skidded around the inside of his cranium, tearing up his brain as it went.

Dean Shipley fell forward, his body sliding a few inches through the leaf litter before coming to rest.

Chapter Two

MY SISTER AND I pulled into the parking lot of the Golden Years assisted living facility. I let her drive my new 2019 Nissan Leaf because she was better at signing while driving. We're fraternal twins, and while I have normal hearing, she's deaf. Another difference is our appearance. We're both forty-four, but Carly, a freelance journalist, could pass for late thirties, while I could pass for ... forty-four. She could star in commercials for hair products, with thick, golden hair that falls to her shoulder blades. My hair is thick, too, but only in an ever-shrinking peninsula on the top of my head. She has a peaches and cream complexion with dimples, while I have more of an aged leather complexion with crow's feet. It works for me—people say I look smart, which is a good thing for a lawyer.

Soon after we were born, our parents learned American Sign Language and relocated the family to Redwood Point, home of the world-famous Bizet University for the deaf. Carly and I have the kind of bond enjoyed only by twins and soulmates.

I'm always nervous when she drives but not because she uses her hands to talk. The sign I use most when she's at the wheel involves holding my left arm out toward the dashboard and sliding my right hand back along my forearm: "Slow down!" The exclamation point comes from the exaggerated grimace on my face.

My relief must have shown when she parked and turned off the car, because she made the sign for "chicken," one hand in the shape of a beak that pecked down into the palm of the other. Her disability makes her exquisitely aware of body language clues. I'm careful never to refer to it as a disability in front of her, because she doesn't see it as such. Despite her deafness, she's probably a happier person than I am.

We were lucky that our dad still remembered how to sign despite his Alzheimer's. He was diagnosed five years earlier, at age seventy. Carly and I are at increased risk of getting the disease, but at our age, it's only a distant concern. Probably less of a concern for my twin, who's better than I am at not worrying about the future. She's also better at seeing the silver lining in any situation. "At least he doesn't remember what Mom did to him," she's said several times. She has a point.

Carly took my arm, and we walked into the facility. It was the best nursing home in Humboldt County, but even so, a slight urine scent overpowered the air fresheners and pungent cleaning solutions.

When we entered his room in the Memory Care Wing, he gave us both a warm hug. Dad still remembers us but is pretty fuzzy on most everything else. We'd decorated the room with family photos and a wonderful oil painting of Carly and me as toddlers, holding hands.

I've always had the nonscientific impression that when people develop dementia they become either happy or mean. Dad fell into the happy camp.

He sat on the edge of his bed. "How's the murder trial going, Garrett?" His voice had the hoarse quality often associated with old men.

I reminded him to use sign language.

He made the sign for "oops" then signed, "If you get me a copy of the brief, I'll give you some advice."

I hesitated for only a second. "Hey, that would be great, Dad. I could use the help. I'll bring it by."

Carly turned to me with a cocked head and a puzzled frown. When young, the two of us had developed our own sign language, and she gave me the private sign that could best be translated as "WTF?"

I ignored her.

We had one of our better visits, the best part being that he never asked about Mom. Carly waited until we were back in my car before saying, "I'm not so sure Dad will be much help with your murder trial." She put "murder trial" in air quotes.

I smiled. Dad had been an artist. The oil painting of Carly and me holding hands? He'd painted that. My firm, the two-person Goodlove and Shek—I'm the Goodlove—didn't have any murder trials going on at the time.

"Well," I said, "when I visited him last week, he asked the same thing, although then it was an armed robbery trial. I took his hands and explained that he'd never been an attorney. That went over about as well as a bucket of ice water in the face. He was depressed for the rest of the visit."

"So you figured you lucked out and got a do-over."

"Exactly." I nodded. "It was like being able to go back in time and make a different decision. I think it was the right thing to do."

"Absolutely." She turned on the car and backed out of the parking place. "But here's the thing, bro"—she's good at signing with one hand—"I thought you had this thing about lying, strange as that may be for a lawyer."

"It wasn't actually a lie. I simply said it would be great if he helped out."

"Maybe he could paint a picture for the jury." She smacked her forehead, her mouth open wide. "Oh, wait, there is no trial."

"Ha ha. It was a tiny lie to make him feel better."

"No, I totally get it. You did the right thing. I was just surprised because of your newfound obsession with liars. I know it's because of what Mom did, but it's getting worse. Maybe you should become a painter. Lying isn't a part of a painter's job description."

Carly was blunt, as many in the deaf community seem to be, but she had a point. We drove in silence for a while, or I should say without communicating, since all of our conversations were silent.

"Everybody lies," she said. "Deal with it."

"Okay, okay. Watch the road."

"You and Jen hook up yet?" The sign she used for "hook up" was on the vulgar side.

"None of your business."

She laughed.

I'd gotten clear signals that my partner, Jen Shek, was interested in me in a romantic sense. For example, around Christmas, she'd given me an under-the-mistletoe kiss that was more than a peck on the lips. Much more. She was a young-looking twenty-nine, fifteen years my junior. Recently, I'd let her know I was on board for a more intimate relationship, but her response was maddeningly indecipherable. Perhaps I hadn't expressed it romantically enough.

My wife had died in a car crash five years earlier, and I was tired of being single. Was I a creepy old man? Of course, we had to be careful since I was her boss and the firm depended on us getting along. It would be a disaster if we had a torrid affair then broke up.

"There's such a thing as being too careful, bro." My sister always could read my mind. "You're not getting any younger." She reached over and patted my receding hairline.

"Watch the road!" I yelled it out loud and pointed. The car had drifted out of our lane. Carly didn't hear the blast from the logging truck's horn. She glanced in the rearview mirror and swerved, and I went back to signing. "And slow down. I'm driving next time."

She took her hands off the wheel to make the chicken sign again. "Little brother"—she's five minutes older than I am—"you're missing the signs. When Jen came to dinner last week, it was pretty obvious she's into you."

"What, loving gaze?"

"Yeah, something like that."

"She'd had a lot of wine. That was the alcohol doing the gazing."

ASL for "clueless" consists of the hearing world's hand gesture for "perfect" moved around on the forehead. "How's the house coming, Mr. Handyman?"

7

"Slowly." I'd bought a This-Old-House dwelling, downsizing because my two kids had moved out. I was doing some of the renovation myself, even though, as my sister's sarcasm implied, I wasn't especially skilled in the home improvement department.

My phone rang. When I pulled it out, Carly took her eyes off the road and looked at the screen. "Speak of the devil," she said.

I gave Carly another glare, pointed at the road, and answered. "Hi, Jen. What's up?"

"Where are you?"

"Coming into town now."

"Looks like we have a new client. A thirty, six hundred."

"Show-off," I said. Jen's extraordinary memory was scary, especially to someone who had Alzheimer's in the family. I had to remind myself that she was the one who was abnormal. "Thirty, six hundred? Take pity on me."

"Assault weapon possession."

"I'll be there in five."

We parked in front of my office behind an unusual sports car. Nothing too flashy, although if it were cleaned up, it would stand out. There was a dent in the rear. The logo told me it was some kind of Toyota.

Goodlove and Shek occupied the second floor of a Victorian building constructed in 1889. Drafty in the winter and damp when the fog rolled in, it was just right on that sunny August afternoon. One of the leaded glass windows was open. Carly and I walked up the path and climbed the stairs.

Nicole, my twenty-five-year-old daughter, sat at the reception desk working on her laptop. Soon to start her third year of law school, she was interning with me. She has normal hearing but knows ASL. I winked at her, and she made the sign for "grandma." I frowned and cocked my head, but she just smiled and turned her attention back to her laptop. Carly peeked into Jen's office, checking out the client, then visited with her niece.

After pouring myself a cup of coffee, I joined my partner. Jen Shek is the product of a Japanese mother and a Chinese father. It's a good combination. She wore her dark hair tucked behind her ears, which were usually adorned with some kind of jade earrings. The dark eyes that Carly said had gazed lovingly at me also worked well for staring down hostile witnesses in court. Her face narrows down to a delicate chin and lips. Lips that made me think back to our mistletoe encounter.

"Garrett, this is Ms. Aksana Ivanova," she said. "Ms. Ivanova has a problem I think we can help her with."

I tried not to stare. The old woman's appearance could be summed up in one word: babushka. It was Russian for "grandmother," hence Nicole's hand sign. Ms. Ivanova wore a purple scarf on her head, and I had no trouble picturing her working in a Polish potato field in the 1930s. Her face was round and reminded me of those shrunken-apple-head dolls. Perhaps not that many wrinkles, but close.

She started to lean forward and lever herself up, but I waved her back.

"What a wonderful name." I shook her hand. "Like Oksana the … uh, figure skater? Oksana Baiul?"

She laughed deeply, her eyes crinkling up until they were little slits. "No. Is Aksana with A, not Oksana with O. Baiul is from Ukraine. I am from Belarus."

"Sorry about that." I sat. "Has my partner told you how things work with lawyers?"

Jen nodded. "Ms. Ivanova understands that anything she tells us is confidential, that we can't reveal it without getting in trouble and perhaps losing our licenses. I explained what would happen if she were to confess to us that she was—"

"Did nothing wrong." She crossed her arms, still smiling. Her body was as round as her face. I couldn't tell how old she was, thinking perhaps her wrinkly face added twenty years to her true age. She wasn't your typical fat old lady—there had been a lot of strength in her handshake.

I liked her instantly, perhaps because my favorite grandmother had had a similar shape. I'd guessed Eastern European even before she told me she came from Belarus, wherever the hell that was. Jen would know. I wrote "map" on my legal pad, a reminder to look it up.

Aksana's chubby fingers clutched beads on a string, and she tapped one foot against the hardwood floor. She wore a floral dress with a yellow cardigan over it.

I put my coffee mug on a coaster on Jen's desk. "Why don't you tell me what happened, from the beginning?"

"Already told Miss Shek."

"If you don't mind, I'd like to hear it from you."

"Is okay. On Thursday morning, was driving on Highway one-oh-one near … Garbville—"

"Garberville?"

"Yes. Garberville. I stop because had been driving all night. There was big accident in the trees, and was tired. I take five and get out and stretch legs. Walk around my car. I look down. Road is raised up. I look down, and there is something metal. *Chto eto takoye?* I say. 'What is that?' Doesn't look like trash. I climb down and pick it up, and it is gun. Big and heavy."

"A rifle?" I asked.

"No. Pistol. You say revolver? I pick it up, go back to car, and put in trunk. Think maybe I sell or maybe give to police, yes? Then am driving on Route two-nine-nine near Blue Lake, and police car passes me. I wasn't going fast. The policeman in the passenger seat is very young. He is very interested in my car."

"What kind of car is it?"

"Is sport car. Toyota Supra."

"That's your car out there?" I didn't mean to put so much surprise into my voice.

She laughed. "Don't worry. Can fit."

"Sorry, I didn't mean that—"

"You think babushka doesn't drive sport car?" She wore an angry frown.

My cheeks burned. "I'm sorry. I—"

She launched herself toward me like a human cannonball, her hand coming toward my face. I flinched back, but she grabbed my cheek between her thumb and index finger and pinched it as if I were a little boy. Jiggled it back and forth. *Ow!*

With that same deep laugh, she said, "Don't worry. Am not angry. Am just pulling on your leg. To have fun."

I had a new appreciation for the phrase "culture shock." I couldn't imagine an older American woman acting that way. In college, I'd had a friend from Hungary who was massive, boisterous, and loud. He always seemed to be hugging or hitting his friends playfully. Maybe there was something in the water in Eastern Europe that made the people rambunctious. Or in the vodka.

I glanced at Jen. Her eyes were wide.

Aksana dropped back into her chair and continued her story. "So, then they turn on lights and wave at me to pull over. They say my taillight was flickering"—she fluttered her hand—"and ask if they can help to fix. My trunk is held closed with bungee cord."

I knew where this was going. "Did you say yes?"

"I don't remember." She seemed genuinely angry at that point. "I don't think so. But next thing I know, they both have guns out and are yelling and arrest me for having illegal weapon. I told them I just found it. They take me to the jail. I pay the bail. One thousand dollars."

I asked, "Did you notice whether the policemen had body cameras?"

"They look like what?"

Jen brought up an image of the body cams that the local deputies use and turned her laptop around for Aksana to see.

She frowned. "Yes, I think older one had that. One had a black tube on his ear."

Jen showed her an image of a head-mounted camera.

"Yes. Just like that."

"Okay, Ms. Ivanova," I said, "we will look into this for you. Do you own any guns?"

She found that funny and slapped her thigh. "No guns, no."

"I assume you've already signed our contract?"

Jen nodded.

I followed Aksana out to her car. She walked with a waddle, a bit like a penguin. *A bad hip?*

She opened the door and got in. "Ta-da! See? No problemo. I fit."

Barely.

I asked, "Could you turn on the lights, please?"

She did. I walked around the back. Both taillights were on. I called out, "I'm going to open the trunk, okay?"

"*Da*. I mean yes."

The trunk lid was indeed fastened down with a bungee cord. It wasn't as flimsy as it sounds. The cord had been looped around the spoiler, with the hook squeezed closed. The other end attached under the chassis. I unhooked it, and the lid popped up. The normal latch mechanism was bent. The shallow trunk was packed with a variety of what charitably might be called pre-owned merchandise. Junk. I saw a bike pump, a motorcycle helmet, a blanket, high-heeled shoes, and a ceramic goose dressed in a hat and apron. It made sense that she might pick up something from the side of the road and add it to her collection.

The panel over the passenger side taillight assembly was missing. I jiggled the wires, and the light flickered. It was a valid traffic stop.

"Okay," I called out. "Can you come back here?"

She extricated herself and waddled over to me.

I asked her if she sold things at flea markets, and she said yes.

"Show me where the gun was," I said.

"Don't remember."

"Was it in plain sight?" I'd almost asked, *Was in plain sight?* Her speech pattern was contagious.

"Maybe."

"Not in a case?"

She shook her head. "No, definitely no."

"What is your primary language?"

"I know car is messy. Please don't judge. Was about to clean it."

In addition to the junk in the trunk, the tiny rear seat area held bags from fast-food restaurants, some plastic place mats, and a big floppy hat. It was hard not to judge her. It wasn't quite a hoarder's car, but it was close. *Is her house that chaotic?*

"What do they speak in Belarus?" I asked again.

"I speak Russian. Also Belarusian. Most speak Russian."

"So, when you said, '*Da*,' that was—"

"Yes, Russian. Is Russian for 'yes.'"

When she turned the key, the motor started right up and purred like a tiger. I watched her drive away, feeling some nostalgia for my grandmother, who'd died when I was ten. Both she and Ms. Ivanova had a jolly outlook on life that I envied.

Jen and Nicole joined me in my office. It had a nice view of the marina on Woodley Island, and I'd chosen to cover my hardwood floor with a Persian rug. Otherwise

Jen's office and mine were the same. I sat behind the desk and filled them in on what I'd seen of Aksana's car.

I looked at Jen. Since she was only four years older than my daughter, I had no right to expect that she be romantically interested in me. *Should I trust Carly's judgment?* There in the office, her gaze was collegial, not loving.

I opened my laptop. "Anyone know where Belarus is?"

Nicole shrugged. "Near Russia, right?"

"It's between Russia and Poland, above Ukraine and below Lithuania and Latvia." Jen was making notes as she spoke. My partner, the human Wikipedia.

I had Google Maps up and saw she was exactly right. "So, do you both buy her story?"

"Maybe," Nicole said. "You're Mr. Human Lie Detector, what do you think?"

"Hey, you two can stop calling me that. I never said that."

Jen and Nicole shared a chuckle. I'd recently returned from New York City, where I'd attended a seminar on lying presented by an ex-CIA agent.

I said, "The agent stressed that we wouldn't become human lie detectors, but by looking for specific signs we could get an indication of truthfulness. Besides, whether or not we think she's lying isn't—"

"You said there are specific signs of lying, right, boss?" Jen asked.

"Well, it's interesting. If the subject shows one of the signs within five seconds then shows at least one more sign while answering a question, it suggests he or she is lying."

"For example?"

"Let's see, there are process complaints—things like 'why are you asking me that?'—a pause in answering, grooming behaviors, failure to understand a simple question, repeating the question, stuff like that. I didn't see any of that when Ms. Ivanova spoke, but we didn't ask her any direct questions."

Jen looked me in the eyes. "Are you attracted to Jacqui Kirk?"

A week earlier a shapely millennial had hired us to defend her against a shoplifting charge.

I ran my fingers through my thinning hair. "Am I attracted to Jacqui? What does that have to do with Ms. Ivano—"

Nicole and Jen burst out laughing.

"You are so busted, Dad. Did you do that on purpose?"

"Plus the blushing." Jen chuckled some more. "Is that another one of the signs?"

"Okay, okay." I couldn't help laughing, myself. "You've had your fun. She was attractive, yes. That's all I'm saying."

"That wasn't the question." Jen was still smiling.

"Let's get back to our babushka." I rubbed my cheeks. *Was I really blushing?*

Jen looked at her notes. "Well, whether or not we believe her, I expect we can—"

I held out my hand like a traffic cop. "Hold on. I'd like to hear Nicole's impression."

"A teaching moment?" my daughter asked.

"That's what you're here for, intern."

Nicole had taken two gap years off after college. The first year she'd traveled the world, deciding whether she wanted to follow in Daddy's footsteps. The answer was yes, apparently, because she spent the second year interning with me. I hoped that a firm name of Goodlove, Shek, and Goodlove was in our future, but I hadn't brought it up. My daughter is as tall as I am, with long straight hair and a button nose. On that day she wore a black wool top with a white skirt. Professional. She'd had a rebellious period in her teens, but our family had emerged from that with no permanent scars.

"Okay," she said. "I wasn't in on the interview, but I listened. 'I found it by the road' is a hard sell, but the prosecution will have the burden of proof. If she doesn't have a record, we'll be in good shape. I didn't hear you ask whether she used her phone around the time she said she found the gun. That could help if she's telling the truth. We might be able to use the phone's tracking history to support her story. Even if she has a record, they'll need something else to make the charge stick. It will also depend on the registration of the gun. I doubt it will be registered to her, but if it is, she's sunk. The cops probably screwed up at some point, especially if they're young. If so, we might get them on an illegal search. In that case, game over. We win."

I turned to Jen.

She nodded. "I agree. But I'll say that finding a gun by the side of the road is reasonable. A bad guy might toss it out of his car window after a crime—"

"Or if being chased by the police," I said.

"Yes." Jen made a note on her pad. "I'll check to see if there have been any police chases on that stretch of one-oh-one. Also, we need more information about the gun. In 2017, a federal court issued an opinion against California's ban on possession of large-capacity magazines, for example. I'll look into that."

I tapped my desk. "We can put Louella on that and maybe have her find out some more about Ms. Ivanova. Did you find out what her occupation is?"

Jen shook her head. "She doesn't have one."

"Retired?"

"In a sense. She said she inherited money from someone, and she doesn't need to work. She's fallen in love with this area and wants to stay here."

"Okay. What's the timing?"

Jen consulted her calendar app. "The arraignment is Monday, and the prelim should be somewhere in the middle of the month. If they play fair—"

"Which they won't," I said, "if Bella is involved." Bella Rivera was Humboldt's newest prosecutor.

"Maybe. But hopefully the body cam footage will be Ms. Ivanova's Get out of Jail Free card."

Chapter Three

LOUELLA DAVIS, SIXTY-SIX, had the heart of a twenty-year-old Olympic cyclist. That's what her doctor told her after the transplant operation.

The cyclist had been training on his carbon fiber bike north of Redwood Point when a texting driver drifted out of her lane and plowed into him. Although Louella wasn't high on the transplant list, a series of snafus worked in her favor. Like meat in the clearance section at the grocery store, the expired cyclist's heart was about to expire. There was no time to put it on a plane and fly it to someone higher on the list, so it made a three-point landing in Louella's chest. Four months later, she was recovering well. Not well enough to hop on a carbon fiber bike, but she felt stronger than she had in years.

Louella looked more like the grandmother she was than a private eye. She'd spent twenty years on the force in LA, where she'd earned the nickname Badger: She never let go. Louella retired and joined the

Redwood Point Police Department then went private a few years later.

She looked up at the framed photo Garrett had given her after her surgery. The shot on the right was her with her reading glasses on, a cigarette in hand. On the left was a photo of the actress Gloria Foster in her role as The Oracle in *The Matrix*. The two black women could easily be sisters if not twins. Same frizzy hair, same freckles across their cheeks, even the same gold chains attached to their reading glasses. One big difference: Gloria Foster was dead, and Louella was still alive.

When the doorbell rang, Louella took the vape pen from her mouth and brought up the video feed from the front porch. She buzzed the lock. "C'mon in, Jen. I'm in my office."

Her home office was small, with heavy furniture most people would call antique. She continued her research on her laptop, and in a minute, Jen entered the room with two bottles of beer. Michelob Ultras.

Jen put one on Louella's desk. "The doctor make you drink this?"

"Nah, but he's making me cut down on carbs. This has the lowest. It tasted like water for a while, but now I'm used to it." Although she grew up in Hollywood, she still had a trace of her parents' South Carolina accent.

"You don't know why you chose it?"

Louella frowned. "I just told you."

Jen dropped into a leather armchair and put her feet up on the ottoman, smiling. She tapped her bottle with a long fingernail. "This was Lance Armstrong's beer. At least he did the advertisements for it."

"Ah, jeez. No more cyclist jokes, please."

"But you do feel better with the new heart?"

"Make sure you never nearly die, Jen."

"What do you mean?"

"I've been hugged more in the last few months than during the rest of my life. Most people get this look in their eyes, like, 'Aw. How are you doing?'" Louella tipped the bottle up and drank.

"They just want to let you know they care."

"Yeah, that's fine, and I appreciate it, but I'm done with that, and now I'm getting on with things. One friend looked me in the eye and said, 'Louella, do you ever ask yourself, "*Why me*? Why did I get to live and not the cyclist?"' I said no."

Jen nodded. "The unexamined life."

"Exactly." Louella felt that people wasted too much time thinking about their lives instead of just living them. It was better to simply take things in stride without analyzing every little thing.

"So, Garrett asked you to look into Ms. Ivanova?"

"Yeah, but I haven't found much." Louella took a drag and let out a cloud of vapor the size of a beach ball. She'd had a two-pack-a-day cigarette habit before the heart attack. Her cardiologist would have had a stroke if she'd resumed that behavior, but he was okay with her vaping CBD oil, as long as there was no nicotine involved. CBD stands for cannabidiol. It comes from cannabis plants but doesn't get you high. Her docs weren't convinced it was healthful but accepted that she couldn't break the hand-to-mouth habit caused by fifty years of smoking. The new regimen had decreased the raspiness of her voice, in any case.

Jen shook her head. "You know your office smells like someone's smoking bacon in a raspberry jam factory, right?"

"Yeah, I might have the place fumigated to get rid of the old smoke odor. When I get to it. But back to Ivanova—it's as though her record has been sanitized."

"Really?"

"Yeah. It reminds me of a case I had in LA. I was investigating this guy, and everything in his background was … plain vanilla. And some things didn't check out. It turned out he was in WITSEC."

"The witness protection program."

"Yeah." Louella took another drag.

"So you think … ?"

"Too soon to say." The vapor flowed out of her mouth as she talked. "I would have called my contact in the FBI, but if I said, 'Hey, your protected witness is running around with an illegal gun,' it wouldn't be in the best interests of the client. I'll keep digging." She shut her laptop. "So, what's happening with you and Garrett?"

"Really?"

"What?"

Jen laughed. "It's not like you to ask about stuff like that."

"Must be the new heart."

"I thought you were tired of new-heart jokes."

Louella unconsciously tapped the vape pen over the ashtray. "Are you going to answer the question?"

Jen laughed again. "Oh, I don't know. It would be such a mess if things didn't go well. I think we should just go along working together. Or something."

"Shit happens, you know." Louella pointed to her heart.

"I've never even put a cigarette to my mouth."

"You know what I mean. The guy this heart belonged to had no idea he was about to die. Or maybe he did, since he was riding on the freeway. Have you told Garrett about ...?"

Jen's smile disappeared as if a movie director had made a jump cut of a video of her face. "No, I haven't, and I'm not going to."

"Garrett's a good man. Keep that in mind."

"I know. I—"

Louella's phone rang. She looked at the display. "I've got to take this."

Jen got up and waved. "I know my way out."

Louella nodded at Jen and put on her headset. "Vince. What's up?"

Vince Rolewicz had been her partner in the Redwood Point PD. She'd mentored him, and he appreciated it. Saved his life once, too. He could lose his job for sharing information, but he never revealed anything that the defense wouldn't be entitled to. And he enjoyed talking with Louella.

"Let me tell you about this Russian girl's gun," he said.

Not Russian, but close enough. And hardly a girl.

"It's pretty rare," he continued. "It's a SITES Spectre M6. SITES is an Italian company, and it stands for, and I'm going to mangle this, societay Italiana duh technologie especiali, or something like that. This is really a submachine gun rather than a pistol. They made it for the police to be used against terrorists."

"And automatic."

"Fully automatic with a thirty-round magazine, quad stacked. The thing is, it's really heavy. Over seven pounds loaded."

"Too much for a little old lady." Louella took a drag on her vape pen.

"Yeah, I guess so. I hear she's not so little, but yeah, I don't see her lugging around a machine gun."

My twin and I had been estranged for several agonizing years. Her daughter, my niece, had died at the age of eighteen months during a surgical operation that I'd recommended. The episode, combined with the death of my wife, had sent me into a severe depression. It wasn't that Carly blamed me, but it was simply too painful for us to be together.

When we got through that, we returned to our habit of surfing together at a place called Camel Rock. I preferred surfing up in Crescent City, two hours north of Redwood Point, where, until recently, there had been no shark attacks. Camel Rock was the bloodiest vertex of the Red Triangle. The other two vertices consisted of the Farallon Islands and Big Sur. I'd have preferred the great whites did their dining down in Southern California, but apparently they like colder water.

Crescent City's lucky streak had ended a few days earlier when a shark attacked a surfer at South Beach. A teenager was sitting on his shortboard looking out to sea, waiting for a good wave, when a shark, later determined to be a great white, grabbed his leg above the ankle. With a shake, it severed the leg and threw the teen into the water. It came back, but the guy, filled with adrenalin, punched it a few times, and it swam away in search of less feisty seals. Because the Coast Guard helicopter, which makes regular passes up and down the coast, happened to be nearby, the guy was airlifted to the hospital before he bled out. The nature of the attack was surprising. The conventional wisdom is that sharks only attack people when they are mistaken for seals. Usually after one bite of neoprene, the animal swims away. No one believes that, like tigers, they develop a taste for humans. But this one had come back for seconds.

That incident, of course, made me reluctant to go surfing, but Carly argued that there would be more waves for us because all the pussies stayed home. Typical.

At Camel Rock we checked out the break from the parking area far above the beach.

"Forget it, they aren't big enough to make it worth our while," I said.

She laughed. "Nice try, bro."

Five other surfers stood around with their hands in their pockets, watching the waves and speaking in low tones. Without the recent attack, they'd probably have already been out on the water. A fishing boat was beyond the rock, much closer in than I'd ever seen one.

After we'd gotten our wet suits on and carried our boards down the steep railroad-tie steps to the beach, I again disparaged the waves.

"Suit yourself," Carly signed and headed out.

Aargh. I couldn't let her go out there by herself, so I joined her. The waves turned out to be too small for her but perfect for me with my longer board. I got three rides for every one of hers. She sat farther out, waiting for the larger waves she needed.

I was paddling back out from one of the best rides of my life when the fishing boat blew its horn. It was coming right into the lineup. Carly was looking toward me, oblivious. I pointed, and she turned.

Deafening automatic weapons fire filled the air. I put my hands over my ears. Two men were leaning over the side of the fishing boat, firing into the water. *What the hell is going on?* I paddled into shore as fast as my forty-four-year-old muscles would allow. Carly joined me.

The firing stopped. Apparently they'd killed whatever they were after. We stood watching while the boat idled, using its engine simply to stay in one place. Finally, the sounds of a straining electric motor reached us. The cables of a crane that extended over the ship's port side went taut, and the ship heeled over to that side.

My sister and I continued watching, our arms crossed. A form emerged from the sea.

"Ah, jeez! I'm never going surfing again," I said out loud then put it into sign.

The boat had pulled up a great white shark that was half again as long as my car.

The next day, Jen and I had a date. Kinda. I viewed it as a date, at least. We'd decided to discuss one of our cases over brunch. The outing had been her idea, but she'd selected the world's least romantic restaurant.

The Samoa Cookhouse, over the bridge from Redwood Point, was built in the 1890s, back when cathedral-like forests still covered most of Humboldt

County. It was where lumberjacks and sawmill operators ate, and it's been serving family-style meals continuously for 125 years. Inside, rows of tables with red-checked plastic tablecloths filled the low-ceilinged dining room, and sepia photos from the early 1900s covered the walls. The place was packed, and the clamor of conversations and the clinking of silverware blasted us when we stepped in. The atmosphere was steamy, saturated with the scent of bacon and sausages. I had no trouble imagining the scene a hundred years ago, with gruff Paul Bunyans wolfing down giant breakfasts before heading out to a day of hard labor.

It was casual Sunday, and both of us wore jeans. I'd chosen a Pendleton wool plaid shirt, the kind lumberjacks wear. She wore a navy blue sweatshirt with the tails of a white shirt sticking out below it. We sat with tourists on one side and local geezers on the other. Waitresses placed platters of eggs, sausages, pancakes, and French toast at the end of the table, and the diners passed them around, taking what they wanted.

"I think the court will do the right thing on this," Jen said.

We were discussing the case of our client, a Ms. Ruby Preston, who had been the victim of domestic violence. After a divorce hearing, her estranged husband had followed her in his car, driving only inches behind her rear bumper. This went on for miles until he dropped back before speeding up, ramming her, and forcing her into a ditch. Many drivers had called 911 to report the extreme tailgating, and a patrol car had arrived in time to see the final attack. Her husband was arrested for corporal injury to a spouse and other charges. An ambulance took Ruby to St. Joseph's Hospital for treatment of a broken wrist. Hubby had been under a domestic violence restraining order at the time and had been required to turn in all his firearms. He hadn't done that, and the police never went to his apartment to seize them. So, when he was in jail, likely to bail out the next day, Ruby went to his place, broke in, collected his guns, and took them to the police. When she explained where the guns had come from, they arrested her for burglary.

I finished my mouthful of scrambled eggs. "Well, it's not entirely clear what the right thing here is. She did break into his apartment."

"I know you're being the devil's advocate, boss, but she took the guns right to the police. She didn't remove anything else from the apartment."

"She was taking the law into her own hands." I held out my mug, and the passing waitress filled it with coffee.

Jen spoke through clenched teeth. "In eleven years, six thousand four hundred and eighty-eight US soldiers were killed in Afghanistan. During that same period, eleven thousand seven hundred and sixty-six American women were murdered by their partners. Murdered."

I glanced at Jen's head, imagining that she had a computer embedded in there.

"She almost had no choice," she continued. "This guy was going to kill her eventually. Sometimes the ends justify the means."

I looked up at the lazy ceiling fan and scratched my neck. "Well, she had a choice, but you're right that her actions may have saved her life. They won't let her off altogether, but I'm sure I can find a plea deal the ADA will go for. Good thing we didn't get Bella the Fella."

"Don't call her that."

"Sorry, I try not to. It just popped out."

Bella Rivera was an assistant district attorney. She was ugly inside, and the disfigurement of her soul leaked out to her physical appearance. That was my theory, anyway, and my excuse for very occasionally using her most derogatory nickname. The court system spawns nicknames like a riot spawns looters. Soon after Bella started in the DA's office, she was bestowed with the cruel nickname "Bella the Fella." As much as I disliked her, I hoped she wasn't aware of what some people called her. Her flaw was that she seemed compelled to win at all costs, perhaps as revenge against a God who had made her such an unpleasant person.

We left the restaurant, and Jen suggested we take a drive. We headed up the coast and went for a walk on Agate Beach, where she surprised me by taking my hand. "I've never really answered your question about a romantic relationship," she said.

"A relationship? What?"

She glanced at me. "Be serious. Do you—"

"Is it my name, Jen?"

She frowned.

"Some women figure I must be called Goodlove for a reason."

"Yeah, right." She laughed. "And they think, 'I wanna get me summa dat!'"

"It's just a theory."

Jen shook her head. "You done?"

"All done."

"Seriously, Garrett, where would you see our relationship going?"

I thought about it while stepping away from a wave that washed toward our feet. The air was cool, but the sun was warm. "I hired you about a year before Raquel died. You remember what I was like then. I haven't been the same since. I'm lonely, Jen."

"You have Carly, Nicole, and Toby. And you have me as a friend."

"You know what I mean. And it's not about sex."

"Darn!"

Whoa! I laughed. "You are full of surprises sometimes."

"Are you looking for a replacement for Raquel?"

"No. Well, yes, but not in the sense of interchangeable parts. Like a new distributor or something. If that were the case, I'd probably have remarried already."

"It could be a mess though. Risky."

"Yeah, maybe it's crazy. It could end badly for Goodlove and Shek. But on the other hand, we've worked closely for six years."

"Six long years."

I glanced at her but wasn't sure she was joking. I ignored the commentary. "Maybe, as with Ruby Preston collecting the guns, some risks are worth taking."

"I don't think she considered for a second that she was committing a crime."

"Even when she was climbing in the window?" I asked.

Jen let go of my hand and picked up a sand dollar. She blew some sand off it and put it in her pocket. She looked at me. "We're getting a little off topic here."

"Jen, I get the feeling there's something you're not telling me."

She stiffened slightly but said nothing.

"Don't get mad," I continued, "but I've noticed that you haven't had a boyfriend since I've known you. I've also noticed that you have a little extra … passion when you're working on domestic violence cases."

She looked out to the ocean where a line of pelicans flew right above the waves.

I took a breath. "So, I guess I'm saying we can take things slowly if you want." I didn't say, *Or not at all.*

Chapter Four

THAT NIGHT, NICOLE, TOBY, and I met at Carly's for our weekly dinner. It was Toby's turn to cook. He's twenty-one. The meals he produced could be strange because he's a bit off-center. Bipolar disorder is the official diagnosis, but it's under control as long as he keeps up with his meds. I needn't have been concerned: He brought a hearty chicken stew that had been simmering in his slow cooker all day. Nicole baked some biscuits, and it tasted like a high-end chicken pot pie.

Carly's dining room was a treasure with a country feel to it. A wrought iron chandelier hung above the table, and the wood floors were old and rough. The babbling of a brook filtered in through the windows.

"Great dinner, Toby," I signed.

Conversation had bounced between Toby's upcoming photo exhibit, Carly's and my close encounter with a shark, and Carly's upcoming trip to some kind of gala writer's event in Redding.

After dinner, Carly and I were washing dishes when Nicole shouted from the living room. "Dad, you've got to see this. Come quickly!"

I tapped my sister on the shoulder, and we rushed in. The screen showed video of the huge shark hanging from a crane on the dock.

"I've seen that," I said. "Is there something new?"

Nicole kept her eyes on the screen. "They found a head in the shark's stomach."

"A human head?"

"No, Dad, a head of lettuce."

Toby laughed. "Must have been one of those vegan sharks."

That clinched it. I was definitely done with surfing. That could have been my head in there. That very shark had probably been cruising right below our feet.

Something didn't add up. What were the chances that a surfer or a scuba diver had been eaten by a shark and no one had reported him missing? On the other hand, great whites travel long distances, so perhaps the unfortunate person had been eaten hundreds of miles away. Maybe a sailor who fell overboard.

The sheriff came on the screen and cleared his throat. "We hope to make an identification soon, but in the meantime, if anyone has noticed a car abandoned along the coast or anyone knows of a missing person, please contact our office immediately."

"Or anyone who's lost his head," Toby signed.

It's hard to explain, but some things are funnier in ASL.

* * *

I'd explained to Aksana that the arraignment was a simple affair. She joined me at the defense table dressed in full babushka, my new favorite word. I usually ask clients to dress conservatively for court, even buying them clothes if necessary, but the elderly grandmother image was the one I wanted to broadcast. There was nothing deceitful about it; that's who Aksana was. She'd worn a floppy sun hat over the scarf but took it off and folded it into her large handbag when she sat. The notion that she had purchased a seven-pound submachine gun was laughable. It would have been easier to picture Mother Teresa packing an AK-47.

She pled not guilty, and the whole affair took only minutes.

The bad news was that the ADA we faced was none other than Bella Rivera. That explained why they hadn't dropped the charges. A normal prosecutor would look into it, see that the little old lady was no gun collector or criminal, keep the gun, and call it a win. But that wasn't how Beastly Bella worked. The woman possessed the gun, and it was illegal, so Bella saw it as an easy win.

At least this would be a quick case. Win or lose, I'd be done with it soon. The happy-go-lucky European was growing on me though, so I didn't want to see her imprisoned. I'd give the matter maximum effort. The charge was a wobbler, meaning it could be pursued as a misdemeanor or a felony. The maximum penalty was three years in county jail, but I was getting ahead of myself.

Bella is overweight, and based solely on her face you'd be sure she was obese. If she had a pleasant smile, like Aksana's, no one would call her ugly. Instead, she wore a perpetual me-against-you scowl. Her face is asymmetrical, too, adding to the impression that she is always sneering. Worse, the tip of her nose is a little high, bringing Miss Piggy to mind. And not in a good way. Yes, I should be more charitable toward her, but those thoughts flee whenever we run into each other.

She left the courtroom without acknowledging me. Aksana took my arm as we walked out of the courthouse. She bumped against me with each penguin step. It was another sunny, windy day.

"Have you fixed your taillight?" I asked. They'd given her a correctable violation, aka fix-it ticket, for the malfunctioning light.

"Oh yes. I fix the hook, too."

"Hook?"

She made a motion like closing a trunk. "For trunk. The hook."

"Latch."

"Yes, latch."

"Good. The preliminary hearing for the weapons charge is on August sixteenth at eleven, do you have any questions about that?"

She shook her head. "No, you explained. Just to see if I have to go on a trial."

"Exactly. We'll probably meet with you after we get more information, okay?"

When I said goodbye, she pulled me down and kissed me on the cheek. I made the pleasant five-minute walk to my office, thinking about our newest client. I could picture driving over the river and through the woods to visit Grandma Ivanova. In my mind's eye, I saw her knitting by the fire, feeding me Belarusian cookies, and pinching my cheek, but not so hard as before.

I stood in what would become my man cave, a tool belt on my waist as if I knew what I was doing, regretting that I'd bought a fixer-upper. At least there was no rush to my renovations. The kitchen, dining room, and bedrooms were livable, who cared if the rest of the house looked like something on a TV show about renovation screwups? My goal was to maintain the old-world Victorian style of the house by purchasing fixtures at antique shops and flea markets. My current task was to install a three-light brass chandelier. It had sat in my office for a few days until I knocked into it and broke one of the etched glass shades. A little superglue solved that problem.

I was on top of the ladder when my phone let me know I had a text message from Carly, who was at some event in Redding. I holstered my screwdriver and climbed down.

Isn't this your client? she'd texted.

I sat on the edge of the tarp-covered desk. The image came in, and it did indeed look like Aksana, but the woman was on the far side of a large room. She wore a white evening gown and her gray hair was arranged on the top of her head. Elegant but still overweight, she looked more like Dame Judi Dench than a starving farm woman digging in the steppes of Siberia.

There was a glint from her neck.

I don't think it's her. Diamond necklace? I texted.

Yes.

I typed in *Go talk with her* then changed my mind and deleted it. If it was Aksana and she had a secret identity, perhaps it was better she didn't know I knew. I thought of a better way to confirm. *Watch her to see if she answers her phone*, I texted.

I brought up my contacts then dropped the phone because my hands were dusty and I still had a crust of superglue on my fingers. It slid down the tarp onto the floor. I picked it up and placed the call, thinking of an excuse.

"Allo?"

"Hi, Ms. Ivanova. This is Mr. Goodlove. I called to see if you can, uh, come to the office on the fifteenth, the day before the hearing."

"Can call me Aksana. Is problem?"

"No, just routine."

There was a pause. I didn't hear party sounds in the background.

"I mean, is problem with police? Something happen?" she asked.

"Ah. No, sorry, just routine. Sorry to call you in the evening."

"Yes. Can be there," she said. "What time?"

"Nine a.m.?" If I had an appointment then, I could always reschedule.

"Yes. Will be there. Thank you."

I checked the text from Carly. *I didn't see her answer the phone. She'd left the room.*

Okay. No problem. Tell me if you see her again.

Ms. Ivanova had every right to do whatever she wanted, but if she was leading a double life—a peasant woman with a dirty "sport car" by day and a glamorous socialite at night—it was something I wanted to know.

Chapter Five

THE DAY BEFORE THE preliminary hearing, Aksana arrived at our office promptly at nine, smelling of talcum powder and Ivory soap.

I'd reviewed the body cam footage. It indicated that she had indeed said yes when the officer asked to open the trunk, although there was some confusion, and she'd said no right after that. Too late. At that point, he'd already seen the gun.

At a trial, the claim that she'd found the gun by the road might be enough to make a jury doubt she had knowingly broken the law, but at the preliminary hearing, the bar was much lower. The prosecution simply needed to show that she'd probably broken the law.

That morning, Aksana had chosen a white scarf printed with sunflowers. This was no dowager socialite; Carly had seen someone else. She hadn't even gotten a good look at Aksana. On the other hand, my sister doesn't often make mistakes.

"My partner is at the courthouse but will be joining us shortly. Would you like some coffee?" I asked.

She nodded. "I fix." She got up and filled a World's Best Lawyer mug with my Peet's Big Bang blend then added three spoonfuls of sugar. After tasting it, she added some more.

"Does everyone in Belarus drink such sweet coffee?"

"Is good for me." She sat in one of the visitor chairs. She must have meant it tasted good to her, because even people behind the iron curtain knew that too much sugar isn't good for you. She took a few gulps and let out a satisfied sigh.

"Okay," I said. "At tomorrow's hearing, the prosecution will try to show there is evidence that a crime was committed and that it was committed by you. If they can convince a judge of that, you will be held over for trial. In this hearing, the state can call witnesses, but we cannot. We can question those witnesses, however. If there is a trial, the prosecution will have a much higher burden of proof. If it comes to that, they will have to show that you didn't just find the gun, and that will be hard for them to do. Is that clear?"

Jen came into the office quietly and poured herself some coffee.

"I possessed it," Aksana said. "Even if just found it, I possessed it, so does that mean it is illegal of me?"

"No. It's only a crime if you knew or reasonably should have known that it had characteristics that made it an illegal weapon. All you knew was that it was a gun, right?"

"Yes, of course. A heavy gun."

The gun was indeed a pistol, but Louella had explained that it was really more of a submachine gun in pistol form. Aksana had referred to it as a revolver, but it was not.

I put down my coffee. "Right. That will be hard for them to prove unless they can show something in your background that suggests you are a criminal or a collector of guns. That's something I want to ask you about. Is there anything in your past that the prosecution might find? Have you had any run-ins with the law?"

Aksana adjusted her scarf. "Any run-ins with the law? I don't understand. What is 'run-in'?"

"Sorry. It means any problems with the police. Were you ever arrested for anything? Accused of a crime?"

"Oh. No, of course not."

"Okay. Now, in order to make sure the prosecution won't find something bad about you, we had my private investigator look into your background. She—"

Aksana jerked her head back.

"What?" I asked.

"Is, uh, female investigator?"

Was that so shocking? Maybe it was unusual in Belarus. "Yes. She's very good."

"Is okay."

"Good. She didn't find anything. In fact, because there was so little information, not even a parking ticket, it didn't ring true. It didn't seem real. Does that make sense to you?"

"Am good person."

"Even good persons sometimes have problems or complexities in their lives. My investigator thought your background was so unusually … neat that it made her suspicious. For example—"

"Okay," Aksana said. A tear escaped from one eye and rolled down her cheek. She put her coffee on my desk then got up and waddled to the window. The fog hadn't lifted, and even the buildings across the street were invisible. "I had problem, but wasn't me. Was my husband. Ten years ago, when sixty."

"He was sixty?"

"No. Me. I was sixty."

I frowned. *She's only seventy?*

"He was good man for many years, then he got sick in the head. Doctor said early Alzheimer's. When he would drink, he would get very mad." She stopped talking.

"He beat you?" Jen asked.

She took a breath. "Worse." She pulled her loose sleeve up almost to her armpit. I'd expected floppy skin under her upper arm, but there was much less than her figure suggested. Coming over to me, she held her arm to one side and pointed to the fleshy part of the upper arm. She looked me in the eye.

I tilted my head. "A bullet wound?"

"Yes. Bullet went in here—" she turned so the back side of the arm was toward me, pointed, and looked at me over her shoulder "—came out here."

"He shot you."

"Yes. I was running away. Was very lucky. So"—tears were flowing down Aksana's wrinkled cheeks—"I got restraining order and moved away, but he followed. I finally used my inheritance money to hire someone, expert from New York City, to give me a new identity so husband could never find me. Have never told anyone, and if comes out in court, he could track me down. I know he would kill me."

She rolled her sleeve down, and I handed her a tissue.

"I'm sorry you had to go through that, Aksana." I gave her a chance to calm down.

Jen asked, "You didn't notify the authorities of your name change?"

Aksana shook her head. "No, no. Husband had friend in the FBI. He would have found out. I had to do it under the counter."

"I understand." I pulled out my laptop. "Shall we take a look at the body cam footage?"

CHP, the California Highway Patrol, had provided the feeds from the body cams of the two officers: Officer Huff, driving, and Officer Young in the passenger seat. They'd also added captioning for the speech in the video. As Aksana had noticed, Officer Young wore one of the new head-mounted cameras.

I've seen them demonstrated. The camera rests over and in front of the officer's right ear, with a strap that goes behind the neck to stabilize it. A wire leads down to the battery pack with a button on it. The camera is always recording in a loop, storing only the last thirty seconds of video but no audio. As soon as the officer hits the button, it saves those thirty seconds and then starts recording everything, including audio, from that point on until he or she shuts it off by holding the button down. At the end of the shift, the officer plugs it into a docking station, and all the video is uploaded. I hope in the future they will record everything at all times. It is way too easy for an officer to claim that in the heat of the moment, he forgot to switch it on.

The video began as the CHP car came up on the left side of her Supra. Drizzle was falling, and Aksana's car had her lights on and the wipers going. Her passenger side taillight did indeed flicker briefly. We didn't know whether they commented on it, since there was no audio, but we did know from what followed that they noticed it. It seemed they were going to drive by her in the passing lane. That's when Young must have pressed the button, because audio started.

Young said, "That, my friend, is a Toyota Supra, fourth generation. I want a closer look at that baby."

Huff said something inaudible.

Young: "Well, I saw it flicker. Maybe we'll be saving the L-O-L's life."

I'd learned that "LOL" was cop talk for "little old lady."

They switched on the light bar at that point, the blue and red pulses flashing off Aksana's windows. Officer Young waved for her to pull over. To my eyes, a flash of terror crossed her face. I hadn't noticed it on earlier viewings. She stopped her car on the shoulder, and Huff parked the patrol car behind her. Huff went to the driver's side, Young, the passenger side. After she gave her license and registration to Huff, Young tapped on the window on his side. She rolled it down. The audio was a little hard to understand with traffic whooshing by on the wet road, but the captioning made the words clear. I'd listened many times and had no reason to doubt the transcript.

Young: "You have a nice car, ma'am, but there seems to be a problem with your taillight. It may be a loose wire. Okay if I open the trunk to see if I can fix it for you?"

Aksana said, with a zeal that seemed out of place, "Yes!"

She turned to Huff when he handed her documents back to her. Then she spun around after Young unhitched the bungee cord and opened the trunk. "No, no. Said no!"

"Stop the tape!" Aksana yelled, making me jump.

I clicked pause.

"I know what happened," she said and explained it to us.

The preliminary hearing was in Courtroom 2, which had seating for only forty spectators. An illegal weapons charge was no big deal, and most of the seats were empty. I counted about ten unhappy defendants waiting their turn.

Aksana, Jen, and I sat in the courtroom's blue theater-style seats.

For years, the Humboldt County courtrooms had been slated for renovation, but it was always put off. The carpet was worn and the wood surfaces, scratched. It had a faint odor of marijuana and mold. The room was much less ornate than the courtrooms you see on TV. Utilitarian. The judge's bench, like the wainscoting, was a light maple, and acoustic tiles in the ceiling kept things quiet, especially noticeable after entering from the bustling, echoey hallway.

When our turn came, Jen and I led Aksana past the rail and to the defense table. The rail, also known as the bar, separates the spectator area from the well of the courtroom—the area that includes the attorney tables, the judge's bench, and the witness stand.

Bella hurried up the aisle, looking directly at me but not acknowledging my presence. She banged a thick stack of folders on the prosecution table and put a pencil in her mouth. I heard she went through two pencils a day, chewing on them until they looked as though they'd been used for target practice at a miniature firing range. Some said that in private she actually chewed and swallowed them like licorice sticks. She wore a black blazer over a brown top and a gold necklace.

After the clerk announced the case number, Judge Nathaniel Ulrich looked up from his papers.

Ulrich was in his sixties and had a perpetual look of surprise on his narrow face. I suspected he had some kind of thyroid problem that caused the whites of his eyes to show all the way around his irises. His mouth often hung open, like that of an old man napping in a hammock, adding to his look of shock. Despite his appearance he was one of our better judges, and I respected his intellect and impartiality. Maybe that's why no one had given him a nickname. Or maybe no one could come up with a rhyme for "Ulrich."

He cleared his throat. "Would counsel state their appearances, please?"

"Good morning, Your Honor. Bella Rivera for the People."

"Garrett Goodlove and Jen Shek for the defendant."

"Welcome," he said. "Ms. Ivanova, have your attorneys explained that we are here today only to determine whether this matter should go to trial? We are not determining guilt or innocence today."

Aksana looked at me. I nodded.

"Yes, sir," she said.

"Good. Ms. Rivera, are you ready to call your first witness?"

"The People call Officer Victor Huff, Your Honor."

Officer Huff came into the well, took the oath, and sat in the witness box. He wore the tan uniform of the highway patrol, and I thought he looked familiar. *Ah, yes.* The local paper had run a human interest story with a picture of him holding a tiny fawn. The dehydrated animal had been lying next to the freeway, but he got it to drink water from a cup and took it to a wildlife rescue organization.

Bella walked up to the podium. Because she'd grown up on the mean streets of New York City, she always sounded a bit like a mobster to me. "Officer Huff, can you tell us about the traffic stop of Ms. Aksana Ivanova on the evening of August first?" With her accent, "officer" came out like "awfisa."

He led us through the stop, the events matching the body cam footage exactly.

We had no questions for him.

Bella next brought up Huff's partner, Rick Young. Officer Young was only twenty-two, still within the one-year probationary period for new officers. He had a muscular build and a flattop haircut. She guided him through the same events but from his perspective.

Having laid the foundation for the video, Bella said, "I'd like to introduce People's Exhibit one, the body cam footage for this traffic stop and arrest."

We didn't object, and the plasma screen on one side of the courtroom flickered to life. We all watched the video I had become so familiar with. When we got to the part where Aksana consented to having Officer Young open the trunk, she stiffened. I put my hand on her forearm, which was surprisingly muscular.

In the video, when Young saw the pistol, he yelled, "Gun!" Both officers drew their weapons and instructed Ms. Ivanova to hold her hands out the window. Standing back, they had her step from the vehicle, waddle backwards toward them, get on her knees, and cross her ankles. Huff "hooked her up," cop speak for handcuffing her.

Bella sat, and Judge Ulrich looked at me.

I stood, walked to the lectern, and addressed the technician. "Can you cue the tape to the six-minute mark and play it without the subtitles, please?" I'd been glad to find that the captioning hadn't been burned into the video itself. It was on a separate track as with commercial DVDs, so the subtitling could be switched off.

He did so, and the video played.

On the screen, Young had gotten to "there seems to be a problem with your taillight. It may be a loose wire. Okay if I open the trunk to see if I can fix it for you?"

Aksana's reply wasn't nearly as unmistakable without subtitles, but it certainly sounded like "yes." On the other hand, the tone was all wrong. Like, *Yes! You must open the trunk!*

I looked around the courtroom. No one got it.

"Officer Young, do you speak Russian?" The conventional wisdom is that you never ask a question to which you don't know the answer, but the chances that this guy spoke Russian were minuscule.

"Uh, no." He laughed. "Of course not."

"No Russian words at all? Russian is the language that Ms. Ivanova speaks."

With a big smile, he held out a fist as if clutching a big stein of beer. "*Nastrovia!*"

I smiled back. "Very good. I'd forgotten that word. What does it mean?"

"Well, I don't really know, but I think it means, like, 'cheers.' Like a toast, you know? *Nastrovia!*"

"Do you know any other Russian words?"

"Not really. Everyone knows that 'yes' is *da* and 'no' is …" He froze, staring at the back wall.

"Without objection, I'd like the record to show that Officer Young is blushing."

Bella said nothing.

"What were you about to say, Officer Young?"

He'd lost all his enthusiasm. "The word for 'no' is *nyet*."

The judge looked surprised, but he always did.

"I'm sorry," I said, "could you speak up?"

Bella stood. "Objection. Asked and answered. We could hear what he said."

"Overruled." Ulrich shook his head. "He said it very quietly."

Young took a breath. "I think the Russian word for 'no' is *nyet*."

"Thank you. I would like to introduce Defense Exhibit one."

Our exhibit was the same video, but I'd had my tech consultant add our own subtitles, the only difference was that Aksana's exclamation was captioned with "*Nyet!*" rather than "Yes!" With that, I was sure every person in the courtroom was convinced she'd answered in the negative. The emphasis on the word now made sense, whereas before it had not. That is, she was saying, *No! You may NOT open my trunk.*

Bella stood. "This is ridiculous, Your Honor. Our officers shouldn't need to understand multiple languages to make a traffic stop."

"And yet, Your Honor, Officer Young admitted to knowing the Russian word for 'no,' and no one looks more Russian than Ms.—"

"Oh, give me a break, Goodlove."

Ulrich brought the gavel down almost hard enough to break the handle. "Ms. Rivera, you will not address counsel directly. Once more, and I'll hold you in contempt."

"I'm sorry, Your Honor. There's no way he could have interpreted what she said as Russian, especially in the heat of the moment."

"Your Honor, there was no 'heat of the moment.' At that point they were making a traffic stop ostensibly to cite her for a broken taillight, but in actuality it was so Officer Young could—and I'm quoting from the video —'get a closer look at that baby,' referring to the car."

"Do you have any case law to cite?" the judge asked.

I sat and Jen took the lectern. "Your honor, in State v. Pearson, 348 N.C. 272 (1998) the court held that there must be a clear and unequivocal consent to authorize a search. Any ambiguity must be cleared up, and if not, it weighs against the state. We certainly have ambiguity here, and in addition, Ms. Ivanova tried to correct Officer Young's misconception as soon as she realized it."

Bella was careful to address the judge. "But at that point, Young had already seen the weapon."

Jen was calm but firm. "If we allow officers to claim they didn't understand someone's refusal, the whole concept of consent flies out the window."

"I assume you've prepared a motion to suppress?"

Jen nodded. "We have, Your Honor."

She gave one copy to the judge and put the other on the prosecution table. We had stayed up all night preparing it.

"Do you have more witnesses, Ms. Rivera?"

"I do, Your Honor."

The hearing continued. The state called a firearms expert to explain that the weapon was illegal and why. However, the revelations about the traffic stop took the wind out of the prosecution's sails. Perhaps more important was the appearance of the defendant. How could the smiley, roly-poly babushka sitting at our table possibly be someone who went around shooting a heavy submachine gun?

I figured we had a fifty-fifty chance that Judge Ulrich would rule the search illegal.

Chapter Six

WE HAD A LITTLE celebration in our office seven days later when Ulrich ruled the search and seizure illegal. His comments implied that it was a close call, but since ambiguity must go to the defendant's advantage, we eked out the win.

I'd brought in a chair from Jen's office so she, Carly, Nicole, Aksana, and I all had somewhere to sit. It hadn't been a big case, but my policy is that all wins should be celebrated. Aksana rejected the bottle of champagne I'd purchased, insisting that we all drink the Belaya Rus vodka she'd brought.

"From old country!" she announced, pouring it into our glasses and mugs then holding up the bottle. *"Nastrovia!"* She drank directly from the bottle. Her toast sounded more like *nas da rovia*.

Carly found it difficult to speech-read Aksana, but Nicole and I translated while our Belarusian guest related a fairy tale about a frog princess who wasn't who everyone thought she was.

I got the impression that if Aksana had her way, we'd continue drinking until we all lay comatose on my Persian rug. Since I'm extremely susceptible to hangovers, I only sipped my drink. My doctor thinks my problem is related to the immune system somehow. I'm fine as long as I don't drink too much. Aksana failed to cajole me into getting drunk.

Before Aksana left, she asked me something that made me wonder about both her innocence and her sanity. She held my hand in an iron grip. "Garrett, when do I get gun back?"

I wasn't sure she was joking, but I explained that since the weapon was illegal, they would not be giving it back. "If they did give it to you," I said, "they would immediately arrest you for possession of an illegal weapon."

She gave me a bear hug. "Am pulling on your leg."

I told her that I couldn't allow her to drive in her condition, but she explained that she'd taken an Uber. I watched her from the window as she walked down the sidewalk toward the main part of town.

Carly tapped me on the shoulder, and I turned to her.

"That was the woman I saw in Redding," she said.

"Are you sure?"

She paused then shook her head and made the sign for "no."

Louella answered her phone. "Davis here. What's up, Vince?"

"I've got some real interesting news, Badger. You're gonna love it. Or not. I don't want to tell you over the phone."

"I'm in my car now. Shell station, five minutes?"

"Fine."

She picked him up in front of the gas station a few blocks from the combined courthouse and police station. She pushed open the door to her nondescript Ford Taurus. He leaned down. "I don't have a lot of time."

"Understood," she said.

He got in, closed the door, and rolled down the window. "Jesus, Louella, your doctor's good with this?" He waved the vapor away from his face. "What the hell flavor is it this week?"

"Cookies and cream."

"Better than grapefruit or whatever that was last time. I'm worried I'm going to fail a drug test breathing this." He leaned out the window, took in a big breath, then pulled his head back in. "So, you ready for the news? This is by far the weirdest thing I've ever seen while on the force. Or ever, maybe."

"All ears, Vince." She stopped at a red light.

"You know that shark they caught up near Trinidad?"

"Sure. The one with the surfer's head in it."

"Yeah," Vince said. "Only it wasn't a surfer. It was the head of an illegal pot grower way out near Alderpoint. Guy named Dean Shipley."

"Shark gets around. Shipley must have gone to the coast to go swimming, right?"

"Wrong. The guy was last seen on his farm on July thirty-first. He was gone the next morning, but his car was still there."

"Hmm." Louella took a toke, cracked her window, and sent the vapor out of the car. "I guess Luca Brasi sleeps with the fishes."

"Don't get ahead of me. We found a nine-millimeter bullet in the head."

"Ah, so it could be some kind of mob thing. Someone shoots him, then they take his body and dump it in the ocean."

Vince nodded. "Yeah. Cement overshoes or whatever. They think they're home free, but then Mr. Shark comes along, bites off the head. We catch Mr. Shark, and voilà!"

Louella nodded. "That is a seriously good story, Vince. But you couldn't have told me this over the phone?"

"You ready for the kicker?"

"There's more?" She turned to him.

When Vince told her the kicker, she made a U-turn, dropped him off near the courthouse, and drove directly to the offices of Goodlove and Shek.

Chapter Seven

LOUELLA CALLED TO TELL me she had some bombshell information and arrived moments later. We gathered in my office, Jen, Louella, and me.

Partway through her story, I said, "So someone shoots this weed farmer, drives his body two hours to the ocean, takes it out on a boat, dumps it, shark eats it, and we catch the shark."

"Pretty much." Louella nodded. "The body could have been dumped into the Eel River, but the timing wouldn't work. It wouldn't have gotten to sharkville in three days. The bad guys probably weighed it down and threw it into the ocean from a boat."

Jen tucked her hair behind her ears. "That's a great story, Louella, but you said you had a bombshell?"

"Here it is, but I haven't confirmed it yet. According to my source's source, the bullet in Shipley's head was fired by Aksana Ivanova's gun."

Jen and I groaned together.

"Oh, man!" I leaned back in my chair. "Have they arrested her?"

"Not yet." Louella looked at her watch. "I have to go. I'll keep you posted."

After she left, Jen walked over to the window. "The DA will have a tough time. Pretty frustrating for them."

"Right," I said. "Fruit of the poisonous tree." Because the gun was obtained through an illegal search, the prosecution wouldn't be able to use it to convict Ivanova.

Jen crossed her arms. "But they'll probably find some other physical evidence that she was at that farm unless she was really careful."

"Maybe, but it will still—wait a second." I frowned at Jen. "You think she killed him?"

"Don't you?"

"No. I'm thinking that the killer was driving up one-oh-one and wisely decided to throw the gun out of the car. Aksana found it, as she said."

"If I were going to throw my gun out the window," Jen said, "I'd do it on a more remote road. And I'd throw it far away from the road. Or into a body of water. Aksana said she found it right near the shoulder."

"Maybe."

"And perhaps we know she was lying."

"How do we know that?" I looked at her sideways.

"Well, remember the day before the prelim, when she came to the office?"

"Yeah."

"You asked her whether she'd had any run-ins with the law. Do you remember what she answered?"

I nodded. "She said no."

"She didn't. First she adjusted her scarf. Grooming behavior. Next she said, 'Any run-ins with the law?' Repeating the question. Then she said, 'I don't understand. What is *run-in*?' Not understanding a simple question."

"Well, it isn't a simple question if you're not a native English speaker. 'Run-in' doesn't make any sense unless you're familiar with the idiom."

Jen waggled her hand. "Maybe. I have a feeling she knows more than she lets on."

"No. I don't buy it. The CIA agent stressed that we wouldn't become human lie detectors."

"What about the spousal abuse story? Did you buy that?"

I said nothing.

"The story of her husband shooting her? She said the bullet went in here—" Jen held her arm as if making a muscle with her biceps and pointed to the front side "—and came out here." She pointed to the back. "But Aksana said that her husband shot her when she was running away. There's no way the bullet could have taken that path."

I tried twisting my arm so that trajectory would make sense. It would only work if she had a weird running style or if she was hit by a ricochet. "Hmm. Maybe she simply didn't remember it right."

"C'mon, boss. If someone shot you, don't you think you'd remember every millisecond?"

"Maybe she just made a mistake when describing it to me." I sat there tapping my chin. Jen was very persuasive, and my mind started shifting into a new alignment. I remembered some things that had bothered me about Aksana. She had seemed slow and frail, but when she jumped out of her chair to pinch my cheek, she'd made me think of those female East German Olympic athletes who'd taken testosterone. And when she'd walked up the sidewalk after drinking enough vodka to put a stallion under the table, had she been waddling less?

Jen pulled on one ear. "What did you think of her general personality?"

"What do you mean?"

"Sometimes it feels like she's a robot or something."

"What? No way," I said. "She laughed. She had plenty of personality. Remember this?" I pinched and wiggled my cheek.

"But it seems fake. You didn't feel that?"

"Like there was no *there* there?"

"Exactly. No soul."

"Nah. I kinda know what you mean, but we hardly know her. Are you saying she's a sociopath?"

"Or a psychopath."

"Remind me."

"A sociopath has a weak conscience. A psychopath has none. Totally missing. But you're right, it's too early to make that judgment."

We hashed things over, figuring the police would delay arresting Ivanova until they'd gathered more evidence. It had to be killing Bella that she wouldn't be able to use the ballistics.

By the time I got home, I was convinced that Ivanova was indeed lying. I lay back on the couch and shook my head. I thought about the day I'd come to despise lies and the lying liars who told them.

* * *

It had happened when I was thirteen. I was in the Boy Scouts, and my troop was on a field trip to Redding, California, a three-hour drive inland from Redwood Point. Since we lived in such a rural setting, our trips often took us to cities. The theme of the outing had been How a City Works, with planned visits to the power company, the fire station, and the sewage treatment plant.

I had been thrilled to visit the Sundial Bridge because I was working on my architecture merit badge. The bridge is for pedestrians and cyclists only and passes over the Sacramento River. It's a suspension bridge with only one tower, and the tower is angled like the gnomon of a sundial. I knew what a gnomon was because, being an overachiever, I'd studied up on sundials. I remember being disappointed that it doesn't tell time accurately except on the summer solstice between 11:30 and 3:10.

It was sunny and over a hundred that day—something that never happens in Redwood Point. Our scout leader, barely in control of us, had been about to cut the visit short because of the heat. I was taking pictures of the bridge with my Instamatic camera when my best friend, Wayne, said, "Hey, Gary, isn't that your mom?"

"No." I didn't even look, continuing to take pictures that would also count toward my photography badge. "My mom is in Sacramento." My mother had a job in Sacramento and spent five days a week away from home.

"Sure looks like her."

I turned to where he was pointing. *Huh.* It did look a lot like her. "Cover for me," I said and started off toward the woman. I figured I'd get some pictures of her and surprise my family with shots of this dead ringer.

Wayne called after me, "What do you mean, cover for you?"

I ignored him, walking fast to catch up with her. I got a good photo from a distance because I was sure the resemblance would fall apart when I got closer. It didn't. If anything, the woman looked *more* like Mom the closer I got.

She was walking with a man and two young kids. A boy and a girl. I figured they were about eight and ten. She held the hand of the girl, and the man held the boy's hand. The dad must have made a joke, because she laughed. She kissed him and took his free hand.

I was fifty feet back when they got to the end of the bridge and walked toward the parking lot. My mind was reeling, and at that point I'd decided that Mom had a twin sister she'd never told us about. I'd learned that fraternal twins, like Carly and me, can run in families, but identical twins do not. This woman was as identical to my mom as could be.

I got closer, trying to get up the nerve to call out to her. My mom's photo sat in my wallet. I could show it to her, and we'd all have a good laugh. Maybe she could come out to the coast and visit sometime. The family got to their Dodge Caravan and unlocked the doors. I really had to pee and looked over toward the restrooms, but I couldn't let her get away.

With my heart thundering in my ears, I got right behind her and said in a small voice, "Mom?" Tears burned my eyes. I guess I'd figured things out, subconsciously.

She didn't hear me because she'd been sliding the rear door open.

My voice quivered, and tears tickled my cheeks. "Mom?"

She turned. "Yes, Gar—" Her mouth flew open. She clutched her heart and fell toward the van. Because the door was open, she dropped into the vehicle, knocking her head on an armrest. She had some kind of heart murmur, so I worried that the shock might have killed her. Perhaps it would have been better for her if she'd died.

She sat on the floor of the van, her head in her hands. "I'm sorry, Gary, I'm sorry."

The daughter started bawling, and the son asked, "Who is he, Mom?"

It came out that for years my mom spent part of every week with her other family there in Redding. Her whole life with us had been a lie. I blamed my dad for not figuring things out—perhaps he was already suffering from dementia at that point.

She blamed work for missing some Christmases with us. She sometimes called me by a different name. It had become a running joke in the family: *Wouldn't it be funny if Mom had a secret family, and that's why she was gone so much?*

She confessed everything. She'd met the other man eight years earlier and had fallen in love. He was divorced with two kids. He knew about us but apparently didn't mind sharing her. She'd become so used to her double life that she hardly noticed her lies. The part that hurt the most: She chose the other family over us. That day in Redding was the last time I saw her.

Carly had blamed herself, sure it was her deafness that made our family less desirable. I hadn't known what to think.

"Dad! What's wrong?"

Back in the present, Nicole had returned from a night out with her friends from high school and found me in my trance. She perched on the edge of the couch. "Dad, you're crying."

I took a deep breath. "I'm okay."

"What were you thinking about? Patricia?"

Patricia was my niece, Carly's daughter, who'd died on the operating table.

I shook my head. "Grandma."

Nicole had never met my mom, her grandmother. She'd begged to, but my dad said no. When he finally relented, it was too late. My mom had married the other man then died from her heart defect.

Nicole hugged me there on the couch, putting her forehead against my neck. "It was a long time ago."

It still felt like yesterday to me.

"You've made up for it by being a great dad," she said.

I laughed and wiped away my tears. "I'm not sure that makes sense, sweetheart, but thanks."

Chapter Eight

THE DAY FOLLOWING THE news about the ballistics match, the fog returned with a bone in its teeth. It hated those few times when the northern coast of California heated up, and it rushed in with a vengeance. Of course, it was elementary physics: The hot air rises, and the cool, damp marine layer flows in to take its place.

The cool fog gave me an excuse to use my favorite feature in my office: the fireplace. The fire was crackling away as Goodlove, Shek, and temporary intern Goodlove had an argument. I sat on the couch, while Nicole sat at my desk, and Jen paced around.

Jen stopped pacing and put her hands on her hips. "Of *course* it doesn't matter what we believe. You're not thinking like a lawyer. Your worsening complex about liars is clouding your judgment. If you—"

"You're right," I said.

"I am?"

"Yes. With Ivanova, I was starting to see her as a lovable grandmother. A colorful character. Then when you convinced me she was lying, I felt betrayed. But I should be able to put that aside. Nicole, what are the steps involved in thinking like a lawyer?"

"C'mon, Dad. Not now."

"No, it's relevant."

She looked at the ceiling as though a list were printed there. "One, identify the applicable laws, statutes, and decisions. Two, research the available facts in the case. Three, apply the applicable laws to the facts of the case to determine the rights or duties created by those facts. Four, give all interns involved in the case a huge bonus."

I tapped my ear with one palm. "Sorry, I missed the last one, but the rest were spot-on."

Jen said, "And you're not going to like this, boss, but I think it's possible—and don't get mad—I think it's possible that if Ms. Ivanova were young and shapely, you'd be more inclined to take the case."

"Oh, come on. I'm not like that."

"You *are* a bit of a cacomorphobe, Dad."

"What the hell is that?"

"From cacomorphobia," Nicole said.

"What? Fear of witches?"

"Witches?"

I shrugged. "Cackling witches?"

They both laughed. Jen said, "No, it's a fear of fat people."

"Not so." I shook my head. "Except for Bella. I'm afraid of her. And we're getting off track here. Or maybe not. If the Belarusian babushka calls and hires us, we'd probably have to face Bella the ... Beastly. How are our finances, Nicole? Do we have a problem?"

"Nothing a murder defense wouldn't solve."

"Well, I'm going to say no on this one. It *does* matter if I think she's guilty, because if I think so, a jury will think so. It won't help our reputation if we lose."

"Bullshit, boss."

"What, you don't agree?"

"We hardly know anything about the situation at this point," Jen said. "Maybe she has an ironclad alibi."

I crossed my arms. "You say that as if the medical examiner will be able to figure out the time of death. It's not like they could check the temperature of the body or examine the contents of the stomach—and I'm not talking about the shark's stomach."

"They'll get a range based on other factors. Like when he was last seen. Aksana said she'd been driving all night. Maybe that will eliminate her right off the bat."

"Well, maybe I don't like her. She's kind of brash. Life's too short."

"Did she hurt your wittle cheek?" Jen came over and pinched and wiggled my cheek.

"That's easy for you to say. You didn't have a three-hundred-pound Bolshevik fly toward you like some kind of Russian Tupolev bomber."

"Oh, that's just the cacomorphobe talking," Jen said. "And she doesn't weigh that much."

"I think she's cute, Dad."

"Cute?"

The phone rang. I looked at the caller ID. It was her. I put it on speaker. "Goodlove and Shek."

Aksana's voice was loud enough to overload the speaker. "Oh. Am glad I got you. Police have been watching me. Is allowed?"

"It is."

"Someone said they might arrest me."

I frowned. "Who told you that?"

"Friend of friend. Please, can you be my lawyer again if they arrest me?"

"I'm sorry, Ms. Ivanova, but—may I put you on hold for a second?"

Jen had gotten in my face with the hearing-world time-out signal, a "T" with her hands.

I didn't like the interruption. "What?"

"You said earlier that I convinced you she was lying."

"Yeah, you did. Yesterday."

Jen shook her head. "I was just making the argument. I don't necessarily think she was lying, those were your bullshit lie-detector … signs."

I pointed to my upper arm. "What about the bullet story?"

"You were right. Maybe she misspoke when she was relating the story."

"Sorry, Jen. I'm going to overrule you on this one."

"Humph!"

After an instant of thinking about how cute Jen was when she was angry, I released the hold button. "I'm sorry, Ms. Ivanova, we won't be able to take your case."

Some intense Russian came out of the speaker followed by "Would be willing to do lie detector."

Polygraphs weren't as useful as the general public believed.

"I'm sorry, Ms. Ivanova."

"Am very sad, Mr. Goodlove. I like you very many."

I was about to say, *I like you, too*, but she spared me the lie because she'd already hung up.

I sighed. It was the right decision. Why did I feel so uncomfortable?

"Now who's lying?" Jen said.

Nicole was watching but wisely staying out of things.

"I didn't lie."

"You said, 'We won't be able to take your case.'"

"Should I have said, 'I don't want to take your case because I think you're a liar'?" White lies to keep from hurting someone's feelings are okay. Lying about whether you put a bullet into someone's head is not. I simply didn't want to have anything to do with the case.

We sat quietly for a while, then Nicole said, "For the record, Dad, I think maybe she's telling the truth."

Louella's daughter had flown up from LA for a visit, something she'd done more frequently since her mom's heart attack. Gail had even brought Thai food from Louella's favorite LA restaurant. They were enjoying the *yam nua* as part of their late dinner when Louella's landline rang.

"I'm not going to answer," she said.

Vince's voice came from the answering machine. "Louella, pick up, this is important. It's about Goodlove."

Louella put down her chopsticks and rushed into the living room.

Vince continued, "We're hearing that—"

She picked up the phone. "I'm here, Vince."

"Good. Hey, look. We got a tip that something's going to happen to Garrett Goodlove. It sounds bad."

"What, like a hit?"

"We don't know. It was an anonymous tip. We're sending a car to his house."

She hung up and dialed Garrett's number. It went straight to voicemail. There were plenty of dead spots on the North Coast. She called Jen.

"Louella?"

"Hi, Jen, is Garrett with you?"

"No."

"Do you know where he is?"

"Yes, we were offered a plea deal in the Ruby Preston case—she's the woman who took her husband's guns to the police—and he went to her house to recommend that she accept it."

Louella squeezed the phone against her ear with her shoulder while putting on her holster. "Why didn't he call her?"

"She has spotty coverage, and her phone wasn't working. He was going to be up in her area, so he planned to stop by her house."

After getting the address, Louella hung up.

Her daughter, a uniformed cop in LA, had been close enough to hear both sides of the conversation. She put her shoes on. "Let's go."

Chapter Nine

RUBY PRESTON HAD AN overgrown lawn. I walked across it and up the steps to her porch, happy to be delivering some good news. The night was cold, so I zipped up my windbreaker.

The DA's office had made Ruby a generous offer. They knew it would look bad in the press if they imprisoned an abused wife for misguidedly taking her husband's guns from his apartment. The national media had already picked up the story with the misleading headline, *Woman Arrested for Turning Guns in to Police.*

She answered the door. "What are you doing here?"

"I called, but your phone isn't working."

She turned toward the worn couch where the cordless phone sat. "Oh, shoot. I forgot to charge it. Come on in." She moved the phone to its charger.

"The prosecutor has offered us a very good plea deal," I said.

"What is it?"

"If you plead guilty, you will get six months' probation. You'll have to wear an ankle monitor, but you won't have to stay in your house. After probation, your record will be expunged."

"Expunged?"

"It will be as if the whole thing never happened."

"But I'd have to plead guilty?" She smoothed her hair.

"Ms. Preston, you *did* burglarize his apartment. Trust me, this is an excellent deal, and you should accept it."

After a little more persuasion she agreed and signed the papers I'd brought. I sensed she still felt the police should have thanked her for doing *their* job, but perhaps someday she'd see that she'd dodged a bullet.

"No further problems from your soon-to-be-ex-husband?" I held my breath.

"No. But I'm sure he hasn't given up."

"You called the number I gave you?" It was for the domestic abuse hotline.

"Yes. Thank you again, Mr. Goodlove."

I was driving back to civilization along the gravel road, when a set of headlights from a big pickup came rushing up behind me. *What the hell?* I'd seen those same distinctive headlights on the drive from my office, thinking for a moment that they were following me but then dismissing the idea.

The husband. It had to be. *Damn.* I hate domestic violence cases.

I floored it. It was only a quarter mile to Freshwater Road, where there'd be more traffic. My EV had more torque than his monster truck, but he was on me in an instant. He tried to come up on my side, but I moved over into the center of the road. That would keep him from pushing me into a ditch.

He drove off the left side of the road, knocking over mailboxes like dominoes. He turned into me and, as I'd feared, pushed my Leaf off into the forest. It bounced through a ditch and smashed into a small alder. The airbag sounded as though someone had set off a grenade on my shoulder. It hit my chin, knocking my head back and wrenching my neck. Within seconds the driver side window crashed into a thousand pieces. One hand gripped my right ear, another my shoulder. I looked down at the hand. In the truck's lights, I saw that it only had—

"I'm just her lawyer," I shouted. "Beating me up won't accomplish anything!"

What was the point? He wasn't acting rationally. He pulled me out through the window. I'd been wearing my seat belt. Did he cut it? I tried to twist around to see his face. His grip on my ear prevented that.

He smashed me face-first into the car then let go of my ear. Before I could turn, a second person pulled a black sack over my head. A drawstring tightened against my neck.

"Hey, you'll never—"

Bad Guy #2 put one hand on the back of my neck and pressed something against my nose and mouth. Hard. The smell of some kind of solvent came right through the hood. Like a whiteboard marker. It was … was … *c'mon focus!*

Louella fishtailed onto the gravel road. She accelerated toward the Prestons' house, but seconds later saw Garrett's car. "Damn, damn, damn!"

Gail had already dialed 911. She only had one bar. "We need ambulance, fire, and police to my location … standby." She held the phone to Louella's ear.

"We're on Langdon Lane, one quarter mile up from Freshwater Road," Louella said. "Car versus tree. Looks bad. Car is not on fire. Foul play possible. The car owner is Garrett Goodlove. Bring Vince Rolewicz in on this."

Louella parked. She pulled her Maglite flashlight from under her seat and trotted through the grass to Garrett's car. The airbag had deployed, and the window was smashed. No Garrett. She played the light around the interior. The seat belt had been cut neatly. No blood. Just to be sure, she searched the ground around the car. Gail did the same on the other side. No Garrett.

Her phone rang, and she glanced at the caller ID. "Hey, Vince."

"What happened?"

"Garrett's been kidnapped. He's gone. Looks like the work of pros."

"Do you know why?"

"No. He had a domestic violence case. Ruby Preston. He was delivering something to the abused wife, but if it were about that, the husband probably would have just beaten him up. Someone ran him off the road then pulled him out of his car. Looks like tracks from a big pickup truck."

"No leads?"

"No, uh …" She stopped, thinking about the shark and the head.

"Louella, you there?"

"It's a long shot, but have someone check the docks."

"The Shipley murder," Vince said.

"Right. Not likely, but … hey, Vince, can you give this top priority?"

"Will do."

I blinked and shook my head. *I'm … on a boat.* My mind was coming together slowly, like drops of mercury coalescing on a plate. My desperate reality came back to me. Someone had kidnapped me, and I was on a boat. I sniffed. A smelly crab boat with a rattling diesel engine.

If Ruby Preston's husband was the bad guy, wouldn't I have just been beaten or killed? If my body was to be dumped at sea, why not shoot me first? Nothing made sense, but I couldn't see an end point that didn't involve my death.

The black hood was still on with the drawstring tight around my neck. My wrists were bound in front of me. Zip-tied. Ankles, too. The foghorn on the tip of the north jetty sounded, reverberating in my gut. We weren't out in the ocean. Yet. No one spoke.

The boat lurched, and someone swore. A deep voice. *They must be having a hard time making it over the bar at the entrance to Humboldt Bay.* The passageway between the north and south jetties was notorious for wrecking boats large and small. If they were having trouble controlling the ship, perhaps no one was watching me. On the other hand, maybe a bad hombre was sitting a few feet away with a big gun pointed at my head.

I made my decision. Better to deal with the elements than criminals who were planning to kill me. I'd earned a merit badge on crabbing. Most crab boats have the same layout: a wheelhouse forward, a crane to pull up the crab pots, and a deck area aft, surrounded with a rail. Even blind, the sounds of the waves told me I was on the starboard side, lying against the rail like a sack of garbage.

I sat and drew my feet up. Slowly. I turned and felt the rail of the ship. The top was only two feet above the deck. A metal bar gave me something to grab onto. I put my hands on it. I thought about it for only a second then rolled myself over the rail and dropped into the sea.

Ah! The icy water made me suck in a gasp at exactly the wrong moment. The fabric of the hood prevented a big inrush of water, but I had an immediate understanding of the terror involved in waterboarding. I coughed. At least they couldn't hear me over the rumble of the diesel and the crashing of the waves. Some part of the hull smashed against my shoulder. The barnacles rubbed against me like a huge cheese grater. Despite my bindings, I was able to tread water. I listened.

No shouts. *This will work.* Maybe I could climb onto the jetty and hide between some rocks. If I stayed in the water, perhaps the black hood would make me invisible.

I'd been surfing since I was nine, so I knew my way around big waves. On the other hand, I rarely went surfing with bound hands and feet. Or without a wetsuit. The cold was already sapping my strength. *Without the hood maybe I can see the waves crashing on the rocks of the jetty in the moonlight.* Taking a deep breath, I let myself sink as I worked at untying it. No, the knot was in the back and too tight. I'd sunk about five feet when I gave up and undulated my way back to the surface. I tried a cross between a dog paddle and a butterfly, but it didn't work as well as I'd hoped. With every stroke, my head went underwater. I rolled over onto my back like a sea otter and dolphin kicked toward the sound of the waves on the rocks.

A shout reached me on the wind. My escape had been discovered. Good thing I still had the hood on; it would make me hard to spot. *Maybe I can float around until they give up looking.*

No, the water was too cold, and it took too much energy simply to keep my head above the surface. I struck off for the rocks of the jetty, taking turns on my back and stomach. The engine sound changed—the ship had turned around, its precious cargo having dropped overboard.

Non-surfers don't realize how easy it is to deal with a big wave, especially if you don't have a long board to deal with. Just dive under it. Works great when you can see the wave coming.

The hood lit up then went dark. A searchlight. Had they spotted me? The rocks were close. The whooshing of a wave roared toward me from my left. I pictured it making its way along the jetty. I timed my dive. It passed over me. But when I came up, another wave tumbled me toward the rocks. Being tumbled around is one thing. Being smashed against the barnacle-covered rocks is another. I figured that as long as I didn't hit my head, I could be patched up.

The hood lit up again, and this time, the searchlight stayed on me. Shouting. In Spanish?

A wave lifted me, and, like magic, set me gently onto a rock. At the same instant, I heard a crash of splintering wood. Close by. The boat had hit the rocks. Good. Maybe it would sink, and they'd all die.

A bigger wave was coming, with the sound of an approaching freight train. I tried to scramble to higher ground, but my foot slipped, and I fell sideways. Would my head smash into a rock? The wave hit, and the whitewater swirled me back into the channel. *No!* The boat was close now. I pictured it crashing down, crushing me against the breakwater.

Instead, four hands grabbed me and hoisted me up. A fist landed on my sternum. I tried to fall back and off the boat again. Didn't work. Someone pushed me down on the deck and kicked me.

"What do you want?" I screamed.

I expected some kind of answer. Something like, *You're going to wish you were never born.* They said nothing.

I lay coughing on the oily deck. My throat burned. I rested.

"Maybe you've got the wrong guy." I'm not even sure whether anyone heard me over the wind and waves. It didn't matter. What did I expect? *Oh, you're not Bob? Oh, okay, you can go. Sorry about that.*

The swell eased. We were over the bar and out in the Pacific. Soon, the rattle of chains came from the other side of the boat. Heavy chains. Probably rusty. They were dragged toward me. My feet were lifted, and someone wrapped the chains tightly around my ankles. *What was that tiny ratcheting sound?* Ah. Another zip tie. *Damn it!* The heavy chain was snug to the point of cutting off my circulation. I kicked, but nothing loosened. I struck out blindly with my bound fists, but didn't connect.

"Tell me what you want. We can work something out."

Without ceremony they picked me up and rolled me over the side.

I managed to take a deep breath, but what was the point? I sank quickly. I stroked with my bound hands like a poodle begging on its hind legs, but it did nothing to slow my descent. Years earlier, in the depth of my depression, I'd have welcomed this. An end to the pain. I'd thought about suicide every day. Even on good days, I'd wished for a release from my existence. *Too bad I don't feel like that now.*

I bent my knees and reached down to the chain, locating the zip tie with my fingers. It was thick. Unbreakable. Even if I'd been sitting comfortably on dry land, I wouldn't have been able to get free. I pulled and shook the chain. With a little more slack, I could slide my feet out. No, it was hopeless. I was just using up oxygen.

I stopped and thought of those who would miss me. Carly, Nicole, Jen, Toby, Louella. I had a moment of gratitude that they'd all been in my life. Selfishly, I also thought about how the world would go on without me. Everyone else would find out what's going to happen while I would die in ignorance.

Then, a surprising sense of calm took over. Nothing mattered anymore. I accepted my fate.

I kept descending. The ocean was deep.

Chapter Ten

LOUELLA WALKED UP AND down the dock at the Lost Coast Seafood Company, her phone to her ear. Clouds of vapor trailed her like a steam locomotive traveling along a foggy coastline. *I've connected the wrong dots.* Just because the other murder had involved ocean dumping didn't mean Garrett had been taken out to sea. She was on the phone with Edith Granville, the detective sergeant in Humboldt's Criminal Investigations Division. Louella convinced her that a Coast Guard helicopter should take a look, but all the choppers had been diverted down the coast to deal with a sinking freighter.

"No, Edith, I'm out of ideas." She shivered in the blowing mist. "I guess we just have to wait. It's the part I hate the most." She listened for a while. "Okay."

Louella switched off the phone and joined her daughter in the car.

I wanted to take a life-ending breath and get it over with, but I couldn't bring myself to do it. The instinct not to breathe underwater was strong. *The hunger for oxygen will override that soon.*

Suddenly, my feet jumped up, and my knees bent outward like some ballet move. *Have I hit bottom?* My feet continued upward, the chain digging into my ankles. I flipped over backwards and soon found myself rising, upside down, water forcing its way into my nostrils. I doubted it was the path to heaven. I pinched my nose. *What's happening?*

My trip up didn't take long. When my head broke the surface, I gasped in a huge breath. I kept rising. Even with the hood on I could tell I was suspended in the air from the boat's crane. I swayed back and forth with the swells.

They swung me inboard and dropped me to the deck. Things made a little more sense now. They'd tied a rope to the chain around my ankles and used it to haul me up. The whole exercise was apparently meant to teach me a lesson or demonstrate their power, but the ultimate goal still eluded me.

"Listen." The voice was deep. Definitely not a native English speaker, but I couldn't place the accent. Mexican?

I turned toward it, breathing hard and coughing.

"Don't take the Ivanova case."

That threw me. *"Don't* take it?" I said. "Do *not* take it?"

"Do not take the Ivanova case. Do not contact the police. Repeat back to me."

"You want me to *not* take the Aksana Ivanova case. You want me to not contact the police."

"Yes."

Idiots! I wasn't *going* to take the case. Therefore, my near death happened because someone had made an unwarranted assumption.

The snaps of a wire cutter told me they were cutting my zip ties. The chains were unwound from my ankles. The hood remained. Once more, without ceremony, I found myself dumped into the ocean.

"Wait," I yelled. "Which way to shore? I'll die here."

It wasn't as if they were going to stop and give me directions. *Go this way and turn right at the second buoy.* I was elated to get another chance at life even though I was exhausted and out in the Pacific Ocean. I was a good swimmer. On the other hand, the hypothermia would probably kill me unless I could get to the beach quickly.

One thing at a time.

I listened. The sound of the breakers reached me. They weren't that far away. *I can do this.*

With my legs free to kick, I could work at the hood without drifting below the surface. The swells were long there, not like the chop between the jetties. The knot behind my neck was invulnerable to the attack of my numbed hands. I got some fabric between my canines and pulled, ripping a hole. It was short work to enlarge it and tear off the hood, leaving only a necklace of black fabric.

Treading water, I turned a full circle, and at the peak of a swell I located the light at the top of the Samoa Pulp Mill's smokestack. The mill closed in 2010, putting a welcome end to Redwood Point's dirty-diaper smell, but lights on the stack kept aircraft safe.

I struck out for shore, hoping that my exertion would warm me up enough to stave off hypothermia. It was a close thing, but thirty minutes later my feet touched the sand of Samoa Beach. On the shore, I crawled for a while then stood. I ached everywhere. I wasn't out of the woods yet. There was one vehicle in the parking lot, a rusty VW bus. I stumbled toward it, too exhausted to jog. I fell twice.

The windows were misted. Someone was inside. I banged on the front window. "Help! I need help."

It took a minute, but then a hand wiped away the condensation and directed the beam of a flashlight in my face. "What do you want?"

"I need help! I was in the ocean."

The door opened, and a dreadlocked teenager in a pair of white boxer shorts stepped out. "Oh, man. Oh, jeez, you're shivering like all get-out. Jeez. Go around the other side. I'll let you in."

The rear door slid open before I got there. He was squatting on an uncovered foam rubber mattress that filled the whole back of the bus. I was pulled in and stuffed into a sleeping bag, then he piled blankets on top of me.

"What happened?" he asked.

"Long story. I fell off a boat."

"Should we go to the Coast Guard station? The hospital?" He climbed into the front, started the bus, and turned on the heat. "You're still shivering, man."

"My name's Garrett. Have you got a phone?" My phone and wallet were in the pockets of my cargo pants, but the phone was a goner.

"No, sorry, man. I'm Harvey."

"You probably saved my life, Harvey. Can you drive me to my girlfriend's?" There was no one I wanted to see more than Jen.

"You got it."

Harvey asked more questions, but I was shivering too violently to answer.

After twenty minutes, we pulled up in front of Jen's house. The lights were on even though it was three in the morning. I thanked Harvey and tried to give him all the money in my wallet, but he refused to take it. He wouldn't even let me pay him for a hotel—he preferred to sleep in his van.

I went up onto the porch, and before I could even knock, Jen threw the door open and hugged me. "Oh, Garrett! We've been so worried about you. You're soaking." She took my hand. "You're like ice. Come upstairs and get in bed. What happened?"

I shook my head. My shivering had increased but not because of the cold. The totality of my experience was hitting me. I couldn't talk. I couldn't think. I could barely keep from crying.

"We'll talk later." She pulled off all my clothes and dried me with a big fluffy towel. Neither of us showed any shyness. She pushed me into the bed and piled on some blankets. She gave me a warm kiss on the lips, tears in her eyes. "I'm so glad you're okay."

I tried to make a joke, but it came out like "Raar whrr."

"Do you need a doctor?"

I shook my head. Perhaps she shouldn't have taken my word for it.

"You sleep. I'll call the others and talk to a doctor." She switched off the light on her way out of the room.

I yelled incoherently, and she returned, turning the light back on.

She looked at me. "Leave the light on?"

I nodded. I'd had enough darkness to last a lifetime.

A knock at the door woke me an hour later. The police needed to talk. I was okay with that.

Of course, the kidnappers had warned me not to contact the police, but I'd never intended to heed that.

My loved ones trooped in and let me know how glad they were I was still alive. Carly, Nicole, Jen, and Louella. Toby was out of town. They then stood back a bit while I related my experience to the county's top investigator, Detective Sergeant Edith Granville. She wanted to speak privately, but I didn't want to have to repeat my story, and they all deserved to hear it.

The detective had retired from Scotland Yard, and her nickname in Redwood Point was "Inspector Granville." At age seventy-six, she resembled a dowager countess from the early 1900s. Like Ivanova, her face held more wrinkles than smooth skin, but in her case they made her look like an aristocrat, not a peasant. Tall and thin, she had an imperious air, as though looking down her nose at everyone, but her arrogance had been earned. She'd cracked several cold cases soon after moving to Redwood Point.

She came over to the side of the bed and leaned on her cane. "You seem to have gotten yourself into some trouble, Mr. Goodlove."

"If someone had told me yesterday that I'd be naked in my law partner's bed at four in the morning speaking with Inspector Granville, I'd have drawn up commitment papers."

"Naked, are we?" She leaned forward on her cane and squeezed my thigh through the covers. "Tell me what happened."

I ran her through the night's adventure. When I got to the part where they pulled me up by the rope attached to my ankle chain, I said, "They dropped me back down onto the deck and told me what they wanted."

She waited. Then, in her upper-crust British accent, she said, "Which was what exactly, Mr. Goodlove?"

"That's the part I can't tell you."

"Whatever do you mean, Garrett?"

Nicole was translating our conversation into ASL for Carly.

"Telling you what they wanted would violate attorney-client privilege."

"Oh, rubbish. Do be serious, Garrett. Perhaps your life or those of your loved ones will depend on our apprehending these kidnappers." She gestured toward the others in the room. "You are a friend, Garrett, and I would be sorry to lose you."

"Well, they told me not to go to the police. You won't be able to do any kind of effective investigation without it becoming public knowledge, so they'll know I disobeyed them."

"I assume this concerns one of your current cases?"

"That is an assumption I can neither confirm nor—"

"Let us not play twenty questions, Garrett." She looked at the others. "Perhaps you can think this over, and we can discuss it further when you are not naked. By the way, a crab boat disappeared from its slip in King Salmon. If we recover it, perhaps you can palpate it or smell it or something to determine whether it played a role in your little escapade. It is most unfortunate that you could not catch a glimpse—"

"Stupid, stupid."

Granville jerked her head back. "Pardon me?"

"My brain must be waterlogged. I forgot the most important part. I didn't see any faces, but when I was pulled from the car, I got a clear view of the kidnapper's hand."

"And may I presume that it was distinctive in some way?"

"It was, Lady Granville. It was missing the middle finger."

After she left, I'd planned to get more sleep, but it wouldn't come. I tried for a while, replaying my near drowning in my head over and over. Then I got dressed. What I'd been wearing was unsalvageable, but Carly had thoughtfully brought some clothes over from my house. I went into the living room. It was 5:00 a.m. Jen was asleep on the couch. I peeked into the guest room, where Carly and Nicole slept. Carly sensed my presence with that magical twin sense of ours, rubbed her eyes, and signed that she would make us some breakfast.

"I'll do it," I said. Carly wouldn't be good at making breakfast quietly, and I wanted the others to get some more sleep. My energy level surprised me. Perhaps it was some kind of joy at cheating death.

Jen's kitchen was small and modern with stainless appliances and white cupboards. I soon had it smelling like the Samoa Cookhouse. I was working on scrambling the eggs when someone hugged me long and hard from behind. When she'd finished, I turned. Carly. She had tears on her cheeks. She rarely cried.

"Bro," she said, "you may be a dumbass, but I need you, okay? Can you be more careful?"

I wasn't sure how. "I'm going to get you a bodyguard." I made the signs for "muscle," "tough," and "bodyguard."

She signed, "Sexy."

"Done."

When the others came in, I was treated to a repeat of the hugging from Jen then Nicole.

Jen laughed. "According to Louella, there will be a lot of hugging in your future."

"Louella?"

"You've joined her in the almost-died club."

I served up a lumberjack breakfast, to which I added four Advil for myself. Nicole moved her chair right next to mine.

Carly was on deadline, so as soon as she was done, she gave me another warm hug and a hair tousle then left. Time for business.

"So, what did the kidnapper tell you to do?" Jen asked.

"To not take the Ivanova case."

"Not? As in refuse?"

"Right."

Nicole said, "But you'd already decided not to take it."

I swallowed a bite of sausage. "Apparently the kidnappers didn't get the memo."

"Huh." Jen rubbed her cute chin. "Not to make light of this, but that makes things easy. All we have to do is what we were going to do anyway."

"Are you serious?"

"What?" Jen cocked her head.

Nicole moved her fork around on her empty plate. "Dad doesn't want to let the terrorists win."

"Exactly." I rubbed my wrenched neck.

"Oh, come on, boss. Now I agree with Granville that you're being childish. You're going to do it to spite these professional criminals, who've already demonstrated how easily they can—"

"What do you mean, 'professional'?"

"Louella said that the way they snatched you suggested they were pros. They were prepared, with a tool to break open your window, for example. So you're going to do something you didn't want to do so you can tweak the noses of the guys who would have no compunction about killing you?"

"Well, when you put it like that, yes."

Jen took a breath.

I put up my hand. "It's more than that. It's not a nose tweak. I simply refuse to be intimidated—"

"But you're changing your behavior based on what they did, just not in the way they intended."

"I've always felt that no one should negotiate with terrorists, and now I'm going to put my money where my mouth is."

"So it's the principle of the thing."

I fluttered my lips. "Yeah, in part."

"Which you always say gets people into trouble. Don't you think your loved ones should get a say in this decision? Carly, Nicole—"

"And you?"

"Yes, and me. And Toby and Louella and whoever else is batshit crazy enough to love you."

"I'm hiring bodyguards today, even if I have to go into debt to do it."

"That doesn't answer my question."

"This is who I am."

"No, this is who you are becoming, boss. First, you're growing more and more obsessed with liars, and now with criminals in general. Do I have to remind you that eighty percent of our clients are both? Maybe with your new attitude you need a new profession, like basket weaving." Jen stormed out of the room. The walls shook when she slammed her bedroom door.

Nicole and I sat in silence. I rubbed my wrists. "Well, that was a little harsh. What do you think, sweetheart?"

"I don't get involved in lovers' spats." She kept her head down but tilted her eyes up at me.

"Lovers' spat?"

"You don't think she would have gotten that angry if she didn't love you, do you?" She made the sign for "clueless."

"Huh." I stared at the wall. "Out of the mouths of babes—"

"Oh, thanks, Dad. Yeah, I'm a babe."

"Maybe not in the sense of being an infant."

She laughed. "Now you're just being creepy."

After a while, I asked, "Is it creepy that I want a romantic relationship with Jen? She's only a little older than you are."

"Not really," Nicole said.

Not really? I shook my head and started collecting the plates.

"I'll do that, Dad. You're hurting."

I let her clear the table. "Maybe I need to think things through some more. I'd had some second thoughts when I rejected the Ivanova case. Maybe this is a sign that I should take it."

"Pretty confusing sign, I'd say, if I believed in that kind of stuff." She finished loading the dishwasher and wiped off her hands. "What would you do if they caught the kidnappers this morning? Would you still take the case?"

I sighed. "Good question."

"And you should go apologize to Jen."

"Apologize? What for?"

"You're smart. You'll think of something."

Chapter Eleven

I APOLOGIZED TO JEN for viewing the world in black-and-white and promised to reexamine the recent changes in my attitudes. I was sincere. I knew I had a problem. We sat side by side on her bed. I'm not sure she knew the tracks of her tears were visible.

She leaned against me. "It was a shock to hear that you were missing and might be dead."

I put my arm around her and pulled her close. "I understand. I love me, too."

She punched me on the thigh.

Hours later, Nicole drove me to my doctor, who pronounced me scraped and battered but whole. She bandaged the weeping barnacle wounds on my shoulder and gave me a prescription for painkillers. Not too many, due to my history of depression.

My car was totaled, and Nicole took care of the insurance paperwork. I placed an order for a new Leaf with a salesman whose daughter I'd defended in a drunk driving case. I trusted that he'd give me the best deal. Were new car dealers more trustworthy than used car dealers?

I put Nicole and Louella in charge of finding and hiring bodyguards. Inspector Granville had a patrol car sitting in front of my office and another at Carly's home. I offered Toby a free photo shoot/backpacking trip to an undisclosed location as long as he left immediately. He took me up on it.

After lunch, Jen, Nicole, and I convened in my office. Nicole showed me a picture of a tanned, hunky guy with six-pack abs. He was oiled up and held a small towel around his neck.

"New boyfriend?" I asked.

"Carly's bodyguard."

"You're kidding, right?"

"Yeah. That's not him, but he might look like this. He was in the military—special ops or something—and he signs."

"But you can't join the military if you're deaf."

"He's not deaf. His brother is going deaf, so he's learning ASL. It's half price because he gets to practice with Carly. He's flying out from Kansas City today. I told Carly about him, and it's all set."

"Okay." I dropped into my chair and gasped when my cheese-grated shoulder hit the back. I sat forward. "We're going to take Ivanova's case?"

Jen said, "We weren't going to take it before they kidnapped you. We shouldn't take it now. We let the police handle the kidnapping, and we go on with our lives."

I didn't remind her she'd previously wanted to take the case. "Nicole?"

"Abstain."

"Really?"

"I just don't know, Dad, okay?"

"That's okay, sweetheart. I'm voting to take it, so that's what we'll do."

"He says, as if this isn't a dictatorship." Jen wore her inscrutable expression.

I looked at her for a few seconds then said, "There's something else we need to think about. Why did the kidnappers want me to refuse the case?"

Jen smiled.

"I know what you're going to say."

She nodded. "They want her to be acquitted, and they think Lubbock is better than you are."

"Thanks, but the problem with that is—"

"Lubbock is an idiot," Jen said, "and possibly crooked. I was joking."

Andrew Lubbock was the only other game in town when it came to this kind of case, and the man didn't inspire confidence. Was he in cahoots with the kidnappers? Unlikely.

"Right," I said. "So my best guess is that they want Ivanova convicted, and they think Lubbock will blow it either because he's stupid or because they can make him an offer he can't refuse."

"That doesn't make sense, Dad."

"Because?"

"If they don't want Aksana around, why not shoot her?"

"Right. But perhaps this is a safer way to go about it."

"Yeah," Nicole said, "because kidnapping someone isn't dangerous at all."

I held up one finger, putting on my best halting Confucius accent. "But, grasshopper, kidnapping poor, defenseless attorney easier than killing woman who own assault weapons."

"Which is why," Jen said, "we couldn't tell Inspector Granville what the kidnappers said. It supports the notion that Aksana is a killer. And your Chinese accent isn't at all racist." She put "Chinese" in air quotes.

I nodded. "Thank you so much."

Nicole pretended to write on her legal pad. "I'm making a note to study fortune cookies."

"Shall we give Aksana a call," I said, "assuming she hasn't hired someone else?"

Jen looked out the window. "We don't have to. She's coming up the walk now."

Nicole greeted her in the reception area and brought her back to my office. I stood, ready in case she launched another attack on my irresistible cheeks.

Aksana was back to the original head scarf. She reached over my desk and took both my hands. She moved them up and down—a double handshake. "Is good to see you again. I am coming here today because I am hoping you will think again about being my lawyer."

"I—"

"I go to other lawyer, and he was not as good as you." She continued shaking my hands, occasionally pulling me toward her so that I thought I might fall over the desk. "I have very much money and can pay you more than you cost."

"Yes, Ms. Ivanova, we can take your case."

"Oh, thank you!" She pulled me forward, and only by snatching one of my hands from her iron grip and slamming it down on my desk was I able to stay on my feet. I caught a whiff of vodka when she laughed.

When Jen told her what the defense would cost and the amount we needed up front, Aksana didn't bat an eye. "I write check now and pay rest in cash."

After writing the check, she moved aside a track light that I'd left on the couch and sat down. Under her long peasant dress, she wore black army boots.

I sat behind my desk. "Aksana, you told us that a friend of a friend said you would be arrested soon. Can you tell us who that was? Remember, we would have to keep it confidential."

"Oh, no, can't do that." She laughed. "That would not be honorable."

"I understand. Did this person say why you might be arrested?"

"Said bullet in head in shark came from gun I found, but only maybe."

"Maybe?"

"It only maybe came from gun."

Huh. Our source hadn't said there was any doubt about the ballistics.

"That is good for trial, yes?"

I shook my head. "If there's a trial, the gun won't be brought up. The judge ruled that it was obtained through an illegal search, so the prosecutor can't use it." I explained how the exclusionary rule protects citizens' rights by discouraging the state from violating the Fourth Amendment.

"Is silly rule. Is not like that in my country. Am lucky to be here, yes?" She was right that most countries had no such rule.

We discussed the case, but I became convinced that unless the state uncovered some evidence sufficient to tie Aksana to the murdered farmer, they would have a tough row to hoe. Perhaps they wouldn't even arrest her. Perhaps I never should have refused the case.

After our client left, I opened an envelope that had been dropped off by a courier. It was from Bella Rivera. On notepaper shaped like a heart she'd written: *Dear Garrett, I was sorry to hear about your terrible experience, and I'm very glad to hear that you're okay. You're a tough opponent, but I would miss you if you were gone. Bella*

That sure made me bat an eye.

Chapter Twelve

AFTER GETTING LOST TWICE, Louella pulled up in front of Aksana's house and looked around. It was about halfway between Redwood Point and the dead man's farm. Louella had a tough time finding it because most of the roads were unmarked. The GPS was no help, and Aksana's directions included phrases like *"Turn right at tree that looks like bear."*

Aksana lived in one of those tiny homes that were all the rage. Louella had always thought of them as glorified mobile homes, but this one belonged on the cover of *Sunset* magazine. It was indeed as small as a trailer home but with wood-paneled walls and elegant French doors. Daniel Boone meets Versace. The roof resembled the raised lid of a cedar chest with plenty of glass on the sides to let in the light. And the view.

Her home looked out over the Eel River and the valley beyond. Not another house in sight. Louella had often thought about retiring in a spot like that. *If I lived here, I'd never leave.*

Aksana stood in the doorway waving, and Louella waved back. They met halfway up the path, where Aksana took both of Louella's hands in hers and squeezed them. *Ow.*

"Garrett said would have many questions. I have made a dinner you will like. Borscht. You know it, maybe? We eat outside. Please call me Aksana. I call you Louella?"

"Yes, Louella is fine. You have a great view here, Aksana."

Aksana gave her a tour of the house, which had been cleverly designed to make the most of the limited storage areas. It was like the interior of a boat with cabinets and hidey-holes that used the space efficiently. The place was scrupulously clean, unlike her car.

They ate outside on the deck surrounded by the sounds of birds and insects. Dinner was borscht plus some potato pancakes stuffed with sausage. Delicious and exotic. Louella asked for the recipes. A chilled bottle of vodka sat on the table, with Aksana taking shots now and then. Louella had one or two—more than that would have made it impossible for her to find her way home.

After dinner, the two women watched the sunset, Aksana smoking her cigarillos, and Louella, her vape pen. Even though she was enjoying herself, it was time to get to work. "Tell me about your life in Belarus."

Some of Aksana's good cheer evaporated. "Was hard life. When child, worked every day in salt mine."

Louella almost chuckled before realizing it wasn't a joke.

"Both parents died in accident at farm. I was nine. 1958. I belonged to state." Aksana seemed to be in a trance.

"We can talk about something else if—"

"Maybe made me healthy. Salt mine is now tourist attraction. Is true. People go down to be healthy. So maybe was gold lining for me, yes? Did you grow up in ghetto?"

"Uh, not really." Louella was raised in a bad area of Hollywood.

"Is okay to ask?"

"Perfectly okay."

"But I ran away when was sixteen. I was very pretty then—I know is hard to believe—and worked as prostitute then joined army." She recounted a severe existence with more low points than high.

"You said your husband shot you."

"Second husband, yes. First husband died at Chernobyl. Second husband bring me here to America, but he wasn't a good man. I show you the scar."

Louella examined it. The wound was an old one, and it was impossible to see which was the entrance and which was the exit wound. "Garrett said the bullet went in the front, but you said you were running away."

"Ah, I see. Is okay you check. I run fast by my husband to get to door. He shoots kind of from side, and my arm was back. Bullet misses my body, but goes through arm."

"That makes sense. Let's talk about where you were when Dean Shipley was killed."

Aksana had been down in the Bay Area but not with anyone in particular. Louella made notes on that and other relevant details.

The Belarusian had downed seven shots of vodka by Louella's count, more than enough to loosen anyone's tongue. However, her stories were consistent and suggested nothing other than a tough foreigner with a surprisingly good outlook on life. She seemed confident she would be acquitted or perhaps not even arrested.

"Wasn't there," Aksana said with crossed arms, "so how could prove I was?"

Louella left at ten, but when she got to the tree that looked like a bear, she realized she'd forgotten her favorite vape pen. Going up the road back to Aksana's house, the lights on the deck showed the Belarusian clearing away the dinner dishes. At precisely that moment, something rushed from the forest at the side of the house. *An animal?* No. A man.

Louella stepped on it, but kept an eye on the action. The man jabbed something into Aksana's side, and at the same time he grabbed her hair and pulled back. Aksana spun around and smashed a hammer blow into the man's temple. He went down hard. Louella drew her gun and fired a shot out the car window into the air. Warning shots were discouraged at LAPD, but this was a special case. And anyway, she wasn't on the force anymore. She had to tell the attacker right away that the fight was over. If he got up, he'd be facing a bullet.

He made the right choice, rolled off the deck, and ran into the trees.

Louella drove right up the footpath to the house while undoing her seat belt. She jumped from the car, gun in hand. The attacker was gone. She was tempted to shoot wildly in his direction, but that would complicate the police report.

The wound turned out to be not in Aksana's side but in her upper arm—a slice rather than a stab. It wasn't deep, but it had bled a lot. Louella got the first aid kit from her car, photographed the wound, and then wrapped the arm in gauze. She picked up her phone again.

"Do not call police, please," Aksana said.

"Why not?"

"Do not like to get police involved."

"Do you know who that was?"

"No, I don't." Aksana seemed more angry than scared.

"I have to call the police, Aksana."

A sheriff's deputy and an ambulance arrived ninety minutes later. Louella left an hour after that and filled out a report at the sheriff's station. The next day she filled Garrett in on what she'd seen. She also mentioned the smudges, like fingerprints, at the end of one board in the floor of Aksana's house. The smudges that suggested she had a secret hiding place.

The police arrested Aksana four days after she was attacked on her deck. The arraignment was held the day after that. Judge Thomas was one of the oldest justices in California, clocking in at eighty-eight. Although he spoke slowly, his mind was sharp. He had a tendency to deny bail, which worried me.

The American judicial system stresses that defendants are innocent until proven guilty, but if someone can't afford bail, they could spend many months in jail awaiting trial for an offense they didn't commit. I once took a pro bono case for an indigent client who had made the mistake of taking his pistol with him when complaining to his neighbors about noise. After the argument had run its course, my client's gun went off accidentally in the hallway of the apartment building. Although security camera footage showed the accidental nature of the discharge, Bella pushed hard for a trial, and the man spent four months in jail for a crime he didn't commit. At the trial, the judge accepted my motion for dismissal after only a half day of testimony, but the man's jail time had already permanently damaged his psyche.

Bella, no surprise, requested that Aksana be held without bail. She made our client out to be some kind of international hit woman who might flee to the old country at a moment's notice.

"Your Honor," Bella said, "she has no ties to the community, no family in the area, and no reason to stick around for a trial that might put her in prison for the rest of her life."

I looked at Aksana sitting at the defense table. Clutching her sun hat in her hands, she looked like nothing more than someone's lovable grandmother.

I stood. "Your Honor, Ms. Ivanova has a lovely home overlooking the Eel River and has made many warm friends since she moved there. She's seventy years old and doesn't even have a passport. The prosecution is trying to make her out to be some kind of Russian spy."

Bella scoffed.

Thomas cleared his throat. "Mr. Goodlove, I will ask you not to put words into the prosecutor's mouth. Bail is set at one million dollars."

He brought down the gavel.

After the arraignment, Jen invited me over to her house for dinner. Just the two of us.

I arrived at seven, marveling at the difference a few days made. The last time I was there, I was wet, shivering, and naked. This time, I was dressed in smart casual: a soft shirt that was a few cuts above a t-shirt covered with a dark blue suit jacket. My jeans were worn out enough to be fashionable.

She opened the door and pulled me down for a kiss. It was a peck on the cheek, but a warm peck that was close to my mouth. I could have turned my face to get the kiss on my lips, but not without feeling like a creepy older boss. I would let Jen take the lead.

She'd done her hair in some kind of elegant braid and wore a body-hugging blue dress that exposed her shoulders and had lace extending below the hem.

"You look very nice, Jen."

She always seemed more affectionate after a drink or two, and I noticed that she'd opened the liquor cabinet. Her living/dining room was ultramodern, with white walls and a floor shiny as a mirror. Copper pendant lighting illuminated the table, which was set for two.

I shut the door. "Something smells delicious. Chinese?"

"Just like Father used to make." She took my suit jacket and hung it in the closet. "Would you like a drink?"

"What are you drinking?"

"I had a vodka gimlet."

"I better not. You know me and hard liquor." I'm prone to debilitating hangovers. The last time I'd had one, I almost lost a case. Jen knew that, and it bugged me a little that she'd even asked.

"Well, I don't want to drink alone."

"I don't mind."

"Nope. We both drink, or no one does." She stepped into the kitchen alcove and emptied a bowl of something into her wok. It hissed and sizzled and released a cloud of steam that overloaded the stove's hood.

"I can have a beer."

She pointed to the fridge, and I helped myself. "What's for dinner?"

"Crispy beef and broccoli noodles with kung pao chili oil."

She sat across from me at her small table, which made it hard not to look deeply into her eyes. The setting made all the difference; the romantic feeling was much stronger there than in the office or courtroom.

"Why do you think they finally arrested Aksana?" Jen chopsticked a small piece of broccoli into her delicate mouth.

"They must have found some physical evidence that ties her to the scene."

"Yeah, I agree," she said. "What do you think of the attack?"

I took a sip of my beer, The Lost Coast Brewery's Great White. "Well, it's troublesome. It'll be hard to cast her as an aging grandmother with no ties to crime if people are coming out of the woods to knife her."

"What did she have to say about it?"

I shrugged. "According to Louella, she was totally confused by it. The babushka packs a punch, however. She spun around like a kung fu master and dropped the guy. At least the prosecution doesn't have to know about that."

"A lie of omission."

"Uh, yeah," I said. "Of course. Let's not talk about lying tonight. This food is incredible. You could open a restaurant."

"It would never work here."

I agreed. All the Asian restaurants in town served bland versions of the food you'd get in San Francisco or, I assumed, in Asia. I guess authentic restaurants don't appeal to the rural palate.

"Jen, have you thought any more about … you and me? A few days ago we learned how life can be cut short."

She didn't look up. "I'm still working on it."

I nodded. "Take your time. But if you decide it's a no-go, please let me know."

After dinner we cleared up and loaded the dishwasher. Jen suggested drinks but refused to drink alone when I declined. I said I'd drink Shirley Temples, but that made no difference. The evening might have turned out differently if we'd had drinks, but as it was we just talked shop, and then I went home.

Part of me wanted to stop thinking about Jen and find a woman my own age. I knew I wasn't lusting after her simply because she was young and beautiful. And it wasn't simply because I was lonely. I enjoyed being with her, working alongside her. *She feels the same way, damn it.*

Chapter Thirteen

ANTICIPATING A SODDI—SOME Other Dude Did It —defense, we needed to understand the Wild West world of Murder Mountain. That was the name given to the remote area of Humboldt County that supplied much of the country's marijuana. Each year, Humboldt leads the state in the number of adults who disappear; what the Bermuda Triangle is for ships, the Emerald Triangle is for humans. If we could convince the jury that the area was infested with gang-eat-gang nests of murderous outlaws, it would give them the reasonable doubt needed to acquit Aksana. And who knows, maybe Dean Shipley really had been executed by a rival farmer. Or the Mexican drug cartel.

With that end in mind, Jen and I found ourselves rattling along washboard dirt roads in the pickup of a Ms. Skye Maritz. Skye was attempting to capitalize on marijuana farming in a new way: cannabis tourism. She founded New Leaf Cannabis Tours, and I'd booked a custom, all-day visit to the weed capital of the world.

Skye was a happy-go-lucky thirtysomething with long brown hair topped with a hemp-fiber hat. Her large nose would keep her from landing a spot on the cover of *Vogue*, but she made up for it with a hometown honey face and an endearing smile. She wore the marijuana uniform: a tie-dye sundress with the New Leaf logo emblazoned across the top.

The tour got off to a bad start when Skye told us, "The federal government classifies cannabis as a schedule one drug, meaning they see it as worse than cocaine, methamphetamine, and OxyContin. They—"

"Hold on," Jen said. "Stop the truck."

Skye pulled over to the shoulder.

Jen turned to her. "Cannabis is a schedule one drug because it has no currently accepted medical use and a high potential for abuse. Cocaine is a schedule two drug because in addition to its potential for abuse, it has medical value. Cocaine is used legally as a topical anesthetic during procedures involving the upper respiratory tract."

My human-encyclopedia partner was less tactful than usual. Could it be that she didn't like the big smiles Skye had sent my way?

I tried to soften the blow. "Jen is just letting you know that we're a little different from your normal customers. You don't have to make things more interesting or sensational. We want the straight dope on marijuana farming, so to speak. No embellishments."

We were three abreast in the cab of the pickup. I put my hand on Jen's knee. She removed it.

Skye's tiny head shake said, *Lawyers!* She pulled back onto the road. "No problem, guys. We're cool. I guess I forgot that thing about the schedules. Straight dope coming up."

We arrived at a picnic table at the top of a hill. It had a view of a wide valley. Skye pulled a pair of binoculars and a bong from the truck's toolbox. She took a hit and offered it to us, but we declined. Jen gave me a private eye roll. Skye opened some Tupperware containers and set the table with avocado toast, vegan cauliflower crisps, and organic energy bars. It was early morning, but the sun was strong, and the day was heating up fast.

"Cannabis was the first plant cultivated by man." She glanced at Jen to see if she'd object. "Archeologists have discovered evidence of hemp cloth as far back as eight thousand years BC."

I wasn't sure we needed to go back quite that far, but I went with the flow. I raised my hand. "What's the difference between hemp and cannabis?"

"They're different strains of the same plant. Hemp has less of the psychoactive component. Hemp has been used for rope, paper, insulation, paint, and many other things. It produces more fiber than any other plant. All of the old ships used sails made from hemp."

"Not canvas?" Jen asked.

"The word 'canvas' comes from 'cannabis.' Anyway, here's why marijuana became illegal." Skye leaned forward as though telling us a secret. "It competed with wood, paper, and the newly invented nylon. It threatened the wrong people, like Randolph Hearst and the du Pont family. They lobbied against it, and cannabis was made effectively illegal in 1937 when it was taxed up the wazoo. The government changed its mind during World War II because the Japanese controlled the production of manila rope, made from hemp, and we needed to produce our own, but they turned the tax back on after the war."

Jen swallowed a bite of avocado toast and dabbed at her mouth with a sustainably produced napkin. "This is interesting, but we need more information about the present."

"Well, yeah. Right. The modern story begins in the hippie days of the sixties, maybe you remember that time, Mr. Goodlove?"

"Uh, please call me Garrett, which is the name I received when I was born. In *1975*."

"Oops, sorry. Anyway, the hippie movement was big in San Francisco, and a lot of hippies moved here" —she gestured toward the valley with her arm— "in an effort to live off the land. The problem was that growing enough food to survive was difficult. Someone's like, 'Hey, let's grow marijuana and sell it.' It was a great idea. The climate was perfect, but more importantly, this area is isolated. We're behind the redwood curtain. Few roads, rugged terrain. Things were easy peasy until 1983."

We waited while Skye took another bong hit.

"In 1983, the government started CAMP, the Campaign Against Marijuana Planting. The fuzz moved in with Vietnam-era helicopters and caravans of police trucks. It was funded in part by confiscation of equipment from growers. As a result, the price of marijuana skyrocketed, something that led to the popularity of crack cocaine, by the way. Here's the important thing as far as you two are concerned: The increased chance of getting caught pushed the gentle hippies out, and the high prices brought in hard-core, rough criminals."

Excellent. That was stuff that would play well with the jury.

"What kind of money are we talking about?" Jen asked.

"Well, for example, at one point the price went to four thousand dollars for a pound of weed. One plant, well tended, can produce two pounds. So, a tiny plot of only one hundred plants could yield eight hundred thousand dollars. If you're not caught."

I whistled. "Tell us about the high rate of missing persons in Humboldt."

"Well, it's not as bad as it seems. Anyone who's involved in the illegal marijuana trade, they don't want to cooperate with the police. Maybe someone isn't really missing, but no one tells the police that they've made a mistake. Plus, a lot of people who come here are reported missing, but when they get back home again, no one calls the police and goes, 'Hey, Ted's back.'"

Skye cleared away the food and stepped up onto the picnic table. She gestured for us to do the same. "How many marijuana farms do you see?" She handed me the binoculars. I shared them with Jen.

In the far distance, a set of five greenhouses stood out. We both pointed.

"Right. That's a legal grow. But there are two illegal grows visible from here. One belonged to Dean Shipley. Can you spot them?"

We couldn't.

With a lot of "A bit below that ridge," "No, a little to the left," and "That lighter patch," we finally were able to pick out one of the grows.

"That site has been flaged." The word rhymed with "lodged." "You see, there's a big trade-off between light and visibility. You want your plants to get as much sunlight as possible, but you don't want them to be seen from the helicopters. 'Flaged' is short for 'camouflaged.' The growers plant manzanita bushes among their girls, plus they tie ropes to the trees around the clearing and pull them over the plants."

"Girls?" I asked.

"Right, sorry. Let me back up. A cannabis plant can be male or female. Growers plant seeds indoors in May and move the plants outdoors in June. Then in July they determine the sex of the plants. THC, or tetrahydrocannabinol, the psychoactive component, is found in the flowers or buds, and those are only on the female plants. In the eighties, someone discovered that if all the male plants were removed, the females grew much bigger buds, with more THC. Okay? Where was I?"

"That's why they're referred to as girls."

"Right, right." Skye pointed. "All the plants in that grow, for example, are females. So, growers say things like, 'I've got to go check on my girls' or 'The girls are getting big.'"

Jen pulled the binoculars from her eyes. "What about legalization?"

"Yeah, wow. Legalization is a big cluster, and ironically, it's doing what CAMP failed to do. For an illegal grow, you cut down trees and plant your seeds.

For a legal grow, you have to pay fees, have environmental impact reports, do a bio survey through Fish and Wildlife, pay a county tax, pay the water board —"

"How much?" I asked.

"It could easily be a hundred thousand before you plant a single seed. Plus, with legalization, the price of marijuana dropped. Right now, we're talking seven hundred and eighty dollars a pound."

Skye stepped down from the table. "And here's the thing. There are three eight-hundred-pound gorillas sitting in the wings." She counted on her fingers. "Big Ag, Big Pharma, and Big Tobacco. Can you imagine a farm in the San Joaquin Valley with marijuana plants as far as the eye can see? That's why I think Dean Shipley was killed."

I froze. "What do you mean?"

"Let's go to his farm and I'll tell you."

The temperature was probably around eighty-five as we got back into Skye's truck. Some of the roads we took to Shipley's grow were little more than wide footpaths. We stopped in a dense grove of alders and started hiking. Skye led the way.

"Dean Shipley was the godfather of growing. He had advanced degrees in agriculture and farm and personnel management. And he had an ultra-green thumb."

I squinted. "And that's why the gorillas killed him?"

Skye stopped and turned. "Gorillas?"

"The eight-hundred-pound gorillas."

"Oh, right. Yeah. He was going to go legal next year. He was a competitor. Here we are."

We arrived at a clearing filled with stubs of what I assumed had been marijuana plants. I pointed to them. "So, the police came in here and removed the plants."

"Police and/or rip-offs."

"Rip-offs?"

Skye gritted her teeth. "That's what we call the scumbags who sneak in at night and steal the marijuana that someone else has lovingly raised from seed."

"So why would the big three kill him?"

"Well, I heard that one of the top agribusinesses approached him and offered him big bucks to lead their marijuana division. He turned them down. They didn't want to find themselves competing against him, so they had him liquidated, no pun intended."

I frowned. "Pun?"

"Well, they threw him in the ocean, didn't they?"

Skye took a break to nap in the bed of her truck, and Jen and I wandered around the facility getting a feeling for what might have happened. *Could I imagine Aksana traipsing around here in her army boots?* I found a shed with multiple rooms inside. Some cots had been set up in one. It was neater than I would have expected.

I stepped out of the shed, and a scream sounded from down a hill. *Jen!*

I charged down the slope, crashing through the scrub trees, branches whipping my face. "Jen!"

"Get *off*," she yelled.

I got a fix on her location and ran faster, my heart hammering in my chest.

There! She was down in the leaves, with something brown and green on top of her. A man. Without slowing down, I threw myself at him, getting my arm around his neck. We tumbled together across the ground. Was I letting out the aggression I'd been unable to unleash against my kidnappers? He wasn't resisting much and didn't seem strong, but I wasn't taking any chances. He might have had a gun or a knife. I got on top of him and threw a hook into the side of his jaw.

Two gunshots sounded. Skye stood nearby, her arm raised, holding a smoking revolver. "Stop! He's harmless."

Harmless?

Jen stood and brushed herself off.

Still straddling the semiconscious man on the ground, I turned to her. "Are you okay?"

She nodded, expressionless.

Skye put her gun down at the base of a tree and walked over. "He's harmless, you can get off him."

"He was assaulting my partner."

She knelt down. "Pete, are you okay?"

The man looked to be in his mid-sixties, with a grizzled beard and a pronounced scar on one cheek. He wore a brown parka and a green knit hat despite the heat.

Skye pulled the man to a seated position. All the fight had gone out of him and more. He looked like an old homeless man as he sat there rubbing his jaw, looking down at the ground.

I picked up a pair of glasses, bent but not broken, and handed them to Skye.

I went over to Jen. "What happened?"

"I was looking around, and I heard steps behind me. I spun around, expecting an animal, but it was him." She nodded toward the man. "He was on me in an instant, screaming that I was a gook. I couldn't get loose. He's pretty heavy."

"Did he hurt you?"

"Not really."

"Not really?"

She shivered. "It brought up some bad memories. I don't want to talk about it."

I hugged her. "It's over now." I was a little worried that she'd say something like *No shit, Sherlock*, but she let me hold her. We were both shaking.

After a few minutes, Skye came over to us. "I'm sorry about that. Let's talk." She motioned with her head.

"Don't you want to get your gun?" I didn't want the man to pick it up.

"Oh, yeah." She retrieved the revolver, and we walked away from the attacker.

I rubbed my sore fist.

"That's Sleepy Pete." Skye looked back at him. "He had a tough time in the Vietnam War, and I think maybe he's still there in his mind. He's generally gentle, but something set him off." She glanced at Jen.

That explained the term, "gook," a derogatory name used by American troops for the Viet Cong and other Asians. Like Jen.

"He lives in a small cabin with another Vietnam vet, Ethan, one more troubled veteran." She pointed. "Here comes Ethan now."

"Why 'Sleepy Pete'?"

"Well, most nights, Pete parks his car near here at a view spot, smokes, pops pills, or shoots up, and falls asleep. In the morning, he drives back to his cabin."

The man she'd referred to as Ethan talked with his roommate for a while then came over to us. Skye introduced us and explained why we'd come and what had happened. Ethan was as skinny as it was possible for a man to be without being hospitalized. He wore a cotton hat, the kind with a brim all the way around. It had "Vietnam Veteran" in all caps written on the front and a crossed-swords pin stuck to the brim. His blond beard was sparse, reminding me of cobwebs.

He pinched the fabric of my t-shirt and pulled me to one side. He beckoned me with a finger, and I bent toward him.

"You're a lawyer?" he whispered. The brim of his hat pushed against my temple. He and Pete shared the same homeless-man smell.

"I am."

"I'm being blackmailed."

"Have you gone to the police?"

He shook his head. "They wouldn't listen."

I frowned. "Do you mean that you talked to them, and they didn't believe—"

"No, they wouldn't listen to me."

I finally established that he had not talked to the police, convinced that they wouldn't care.

"Can you help me?" he asked. "This woman says that I committed a serious crime, but she's the one who did it."

I froze. "Does it involve Dean Shipley?"

"Who? No. Someone else. Can you help me?"

This really *was* a dangerous place. I'd have no trouble convincing the jury of that.

"May I contact the police on your behalf?"

"Uh. Yeah. Okay."

I got Ethan's contact information and told him to call me at the office. He and his roommate headed down the hill.

We got back in Skye's truck and started the long trip back to Redwood Point.

"I'm guessing all your tours aren't this exciting," I said.

Skye shook her head. "I wish."

"You're not getting enough customers for your tours?"

"We could use more."

"Maybe you could stage events like that. Like the Wild West show at Universal Studios."

She didn't think that was funny. Neither did Jen.

Chapter Fourteen

A GOOD LAWYER CAN read minds. Jen was interested in me romantically. I knew it. I'd invited her to one of our family dinners, and she'd accepted. Since Nicole was back at law school and Toby was off on his backpacking trip, Carly and I were the only family. The dinner was at my house.

Carly arrived first and sniffed the air. "Meatloaf again." She had a twinkle in her eye. Actually, she seemed a little extra happy, although no one but a twin would have noticed.

"Tonight," I said, "the chef has prepared minced shoulder of beef spiced with a robust blend of garlic and onions and blended with chopped bacon, grated Parmesan, and—"

"And Cheerios." She used the sign for "cereal," the index finger looking like an inchworm crawling in front of her mouth, but I knew what she meant.

"Of course." It was our dad's recipe.

She tilted her head toward the man beside her. "Bro, this is Zach."

Zach was indeed muscle tough and undeniably sexy.

I shook his hand. "Thank you for flying out here, Zach." I smiled. "Hold on. Shouldn't you be checking out the house or something?"

"ASL only, please. Just a second." He walked over to one of Toby's framed photos, looked behind it, then came back. "All clear, sir." His ASL was halting but not bad.

I gave my sister a private wink, and her eyes twinkled some more.

While Carly was giving Zach a tour of the house, Jen arrived. She wore what Nicole had taught me was called an LBD: Little Black Dress. She'd added a black choker or strap around her neck. Whatever you call it, it worked, and it wasn't too formal for dinner. I told her she was dazzling.

"Wow, nice job on the living room." She walked around, giving it the once-over.

Rejecting the strict Victorian look, the one the house had come with, I'd steamed off the red-and-black wallpaper and painted the walls pewter gray. The plush carpet was a darker gray, the couch and chairs, white. Tall bay windows had a view of the harbor when it wasn't foggy.

The door to my work in progress, my man cave, had no doorknob, but I pushed it open and showed Jen how it was coming.

"Well, you're turning into quite the handyman."

"Yeah, I'm slow though."

"No rush."

I nodded. "Exactly."

At dinner, I found myself on the ASL translator diet: My hands and mouth had a full-time job translating the brisk conversation—no time for eating. Jen was careful to look directly at Carly when speaking, giving her a chance to lip-read and me a chance to shovel in some meatloaf. After a dessert of home-baked, definitely-not-burnt Toll House cookies, Carly and Zach left.

Jen suggested we have a drink or two. I tried to read her intent on her face, but she wore her exasperatingly inscrutable expression. Sure, it was a stereotype that Asians were inscrutable, but perhaps the subtle facial cues of other races aren't obvious unless you grew up experiencing them. Maybe if I'd grown up in China I'd think Westerners were inscrutable. It was such a contrast to Aksana. Her face was an open book full of frowns, smiles, and laughs.

In honor of our Belarusian client, we both had vodka on the rocks. Aksana had gifted me a flask of Belaya Rus vodka, bottled in Minsk. After our third drink, Jen came and snuggled with me on the couch and even gave me a kiss. The lawyer in me wanted to make sure we at least had an oral contract.

"Does this mean we're going to ... uh ... pursue the romantic side of our relationship?"

She laughed. "Well I'm not going to be signing a prenub or anything."

"A what?"

"A pre— prenub. Prenup."

"Prenup? You're not saying you want to get married, are you?"

"Does that scare you, boss?" There was a giggle in her voice.

"Not at all. I'll propose right now." I got down on one knee.

She laughed again. "What about the pre … nub— damn—pre … nup?"

"I'm not sure you're in any condition to enter into a written contract, but I'll write one up for you right away if you want. Here on this napkin."

"Oh, Garrett." She leaned back and picked up my drink by mistake. She sipped it and froze. Sipped it again, and her face transformed into a mask of anger. It was so scary that a part of me wanted to reconsider marrying this woman. She threw the drink in my face. "You've been watering down your drinks!"

"Jen, the last time you wanted to have some drinks with me you kept insisting despite knowing about my hangover problem. I just thought—"

"You just thought you'd get me drunk so you could get into my pants. Don't you think watering your drink was a lie?" All signs of inebriation vanished.

"No! I wanted to share drinks with you, but I couldn't. This seemed like a good solution. Last time you wouldn't let me drink Shirley Temples, so I figured it would work only if I didn't tell you."

She started crying.

"Jen, two minutes ago I was ready to propose marriage to you. Is that what a man who just wants to get into your pants would do?"

"Maybe." She crossed her arms.

"Oh, come on, Jen. Don't you know me better than that?" I stood and paced for a few minutes then sat down next to her. "We've been working side by side for years. Have you ever seen me do anything that underhanded? I'm a good man, and you know it."

She was crying harder. She turned away from me and mumbled something.

I leaned toward her. "What? I can't hear you."

"There's something I never told you."

I took her hand. She whipped it away, but I took it again. "Do you want to tell me now?"

She took some deep breaths, and I waited.

"Before I moved here, when I was in San Francisco, there was a man I liked. We hadn't known each another for long, but I thought maybe he was The One. One night we were at his place. This was only our third date. He had a beautiful view of the Golden Gate Bridge."

She paused. I waited.

She looked me in the eye. "Do you know what Rohypnol is?"

"Oh, Jen, I'm sorry." I hugged her, and she started sobbing again. "I understand. You don't have to say any more." Rohypnol had been in the news. It's one of the date-rape drugs and can sedate someone until they can't resist.

"He raped me. I couldn't move. I thought he might be The One."

I hugged her tighter. "I understand. I wasn't trying to —"

"I know, I know. It's just—"

"I understand, Jen, and I'm sorry. You're right. I shouldn't have done it. Please forgive me."

She spent the night, but we didn't do anything except snuggle, sleeping there on the couch. When I woke in the morning my neck ached and she was gone.

* * *

We went into Aksana's preliminary hearing blind. Discovery laws limit surprises in trials by requiring that both sides share certain information before the trial begins. Counsel must provide a list of witnesses they'll call, for example. These rules do more than increase fairness and limit "trials by ambush." They also substantially decrease the time and court costs of litigation. If a trial had to be delayed each time new evidence was sprung on the other side, the court system would grind to a halt. But discovery rules don't usually apply to preliminary hearings. Thus, Jen and I went into Courtroom 4 with no knowledge of what we were about to face.

Settling in at the defense table, I took a deep breath. The room had the faint odor of marijuana usually limited to the stairwells and hallways of the courthouse. I reasoned that a heavy smoker had appeared recently. I was amazed there was enough residual cannabis in his —or her—lungs to fill the entire courtroom with the scent of weed.

Earthquakes were to blame for the utilitarian look of the courtrooms. The original courthouse, built in the 1800s, included wide stone steps leading to the entrance and a soaring tower topped with a statue of Minerva, the Roman goddess of wisdom. The 1906 San Francisco earthquake, despite being 220 miles away, knocked Minerva from her perch, and a local quake in 1954 finished off the building. So instead of soaring ceilings and hand-carved balustrades, Courtroom 4 resembled a large classroom, with buzzing fluorescent lights and industrial carpeting.

I sat between the petite Jen and the robust Aksana. If Aksana was nervous, she hid it well. I guessed after the salt mines and the Belarusian army, a little thing like a preliminary hearing wouldn't faze her.

The bailiff announced the court session, we stood, and the door to the judge's chambers opened. After a few seconds, Judge Stevens' cane appeared followed by her yellow-white hair and the rest of her osteoporosis-ridden body. It looked like she was headbutting her way into the courtroom in slow motion. She disappeared as she ascended the steps to the bench, and I imagined *I think I can, I think I can* running through her head. There was nothing porous or frail about her brain, however. Whether she ruled for or against me, her decisions had always been well reasoned and fair.

She popped up like a prairie dog and cleared her throat. "Would counsel state their appearances for the record?"

"Good morning, Your Honor, Bella Rivera for the People."

"Garrett Goodlove and Jen Shek for the defendant."

"Good morning," Stevens said. "Do you understand, Ms. Ivanova, that we are not here today to determine guilt or innocence. We are here only to determine whether this case should proceed to trial?"

"Yes, understand."

After some more preliminaries, Bella rose to her feet. She wore a dark blue pantsuit and dangling earrings that clanged like miniature wind chimes every time she turned her head. "The state calls Deputy James Lombard."

Dressed in his tan uniform, Lombard was around thirty, burly and totally bald.

Bella stood at the lectern. "Deputy Lombard, can you tell us what happened on the second of September of this year?"

"Yes, ma'am. My supervisor told me we'd gotten a tip that someone saw a bloody rag or something near the illegal grow operation of Dean Shipley."

I glanced at Aksana. Her head jerked back a fraction of an inch, but I doubted anyone else noticed.

Lombard continued, "I was told to go search for the cloth. I was surprised because I'd heard that the area had been searched already without—"

"Motion to strike, Your Honor," Bella said.

Judge Stevens granted the motion and turned to the witness. "Please testify only about things you experienced directly, not about things that other people said."

"Sorry," he said. "So, I drove out to the farm or whatever and started searching. My supervisor told me that the tipster said that the rag was stuck to some barbed wire on the property. That made my job easier 'cause I didn't need to search every inch of ground. When I came to some barbed wire, I followed it along looking for a cloth. It didn't take long. I saw something white, like a handkerchief, stuck on the fencing. It was plain as day."

"And what did you do then?" Bella asked.

"I backed off and called my supervisor. He told me to wait there until the crime scene investigators showed up."

Bella thanked the witness and sat.

Aksana whispered in my ear, "That was not from me. It is lie."

So that was their game. The only question in my mind was whether it had been planted by the prosecution or someone else.

"Your Honor," I said, "this is the first we've heard of this evidence. I'd like to request a fifteen-minute recess."

Guessing at how Bella's mind worked, I'm sure she was convinced Aksana had used her machine pistol to put a bullet into Shipley's brain. Once Bella jumped to a conclusion, she stuck to it like a pit bull with OCD. When you are 100 percent convinced someone is guilty, planting evidence might not seem dishonest. But no, that would have been going too far, even for Bella. Not too far, however, for someone willing to kidnap and almost kill a lawyer.

The series of events was clear. A full search of the property had turned up nothing. A month later, someone sticks Aksana with a knife and grabs some of her hair. He wipes the blood and hair on a rag, plants it at the scene, and calls in an anonymous tip.

Judge Stevens granted our request, and Jen and I huddled in the attorney conference room. We were all business. Neither of us brought up the night we spent together.

"Obviously planted," Jen said.

"Yeah, but how do we show it?" The defense can cross-examine witnesses at a preliminary hearing but can't call any of its own.

"If they call Granville to the stand, we can bring up the stabbing that Louella saw."

I squinted at the ceiling and scratched my neck. "I'm not sure that will be enough to knock down probable cause, but it doesn't matter."

"Why not?"

"Because Bella knows better than to give us that opening. Plus, she doesn't need Granville. We know a crime was committed because Shipley had a bullet in his head, and—"

"Unless it was suicide."

"Not that again, Jen. How did he end up in the ocean?"

"You're assuming he died at the farm."

"Even if we imagine he traveled hours to the coast to kill himself while watching the sun set over the Pacific, his car was at the farm. So, unless it was assisted suicide —"

"I know." Jen checked her watch. "I just want to keep that on the table."

"So, as I was saying, we believe a crime was committed, and the bloody rag is all they need for probable cause to suspect that Aksana did it. We won't be able to refute it without calling our own witnesses."

"You think Bella knows it's planted?"

I scoffed. "Abso-freaking-lutely. Knows and doesn't care. She sees it as a gift from God." Bella was a devout Catholic, and I often saw her make the sign of the cross at the start of a day's proceedings. "She probably knows we'll be able to sow plenty of doubt in the jurors' minds but figures she'll have uncovered more evidence by the time we get to trial."

"You seem awfully confident you know what's going on in Bella's mind."

"It's my job."

She gathered her notes. "Well, don't let it lead you astray."

Back in court, I established that Lombard had searched the area soon after the crime and hadn't seen the cloth even though it had been easy to find.

At the lectern, I asked, "Did any of the other deputies see—"

"Objection. Hearsay."

"Sustained."

I rephrased my question. "Deputy Lombard, if they'd found the rag soon after the crime was committed, would you have been asked to search for it on September first?"

"Objection. Argumentative."

"Overruled."

Lombard shook his head. "No."

"So we can assume it wasn't found during that first exhaustive search."

Bella popped up. "Objection. Argumentative. Assumes facts not in evidence."

"Sustained."

"No further questions, Your Honor."

Next, Bella introduced a video of the cloth on the barbed wire, waving in the breeze, clearly visible from a distance. She had the county's DNA expert present evidence that the blood came from Aksana's veins.

Neither Jen nor I cross-examined the remaining witnesses. Once it was clear we were going to trial, it would have been stupid to tip our hand. I explained that to Aksana, and she seemed to get it. In fact, she didn't seem worried in general, as if she had something up one of her big, floppy sleeves.

Unsurprisingly, Judge Stevens ruled that Aksana would be "held to answer," and the trial was set to start on October 31. Halloween.

Ethan Crowley, Sleepy Pete's roommate, came to my office in late September with his tale of blackmail. His case had slipped my mind, in part because I had the feeling he was imagining the whole thing. He arrived wearing the same grubby clothes he'd had on when I met him in the forest. I shook his hand then removed a light fixture that I'd left on the visitor chair. I put it on a shelf by the window. He sat, took off his Vietnam veteran hat, and rolled and unrolled it in his hands. Within minutes, the whole office smelled of marijuana, so I opened a window even though the fog was in town.

"I lent her my pitchfork, and she used it to cut someone." He didn't look at me while talking.

I sat up straight. This was more serious than I'd believed. I explained about attorney-client privilege, had him sign a contract and pay a retainer, then asked whether he'd contacted the police.

"No, that's what I'm trying to tell you. I can't. Hannah says that I did it, and she can prove it."

"What do you mean by cutting someone with a pitchfork?"

"You know those pitchforks with the really sharp, narrow … metal things?"

"Tines?" I winced at my mind's eye image of the pitchfork in the painting *American Gothic*.

"I guess so. So, I lent her my pitchfork, and she went over to the other neighbor's, the guy that's always shooting off his gun day and night. Anyway, she snuck up on him when he was painting his shed, and she … jabbed him in the butt with the pitchfork." Ethan stood and demonstrated the movement, like shoveling snow or pitching hay.

"Wait a second. Were you there?"

"No, but I heard about it."

"There was a witness?"

He shrugged. "The guy had to go to the hospital, and one of the … tines went into his bowl."

"Bowel?"

"Yeah. His colon." Ethan pronounced it like "cologne." "Hannah said he fell forward, and he didn't see her, and she ran away without him seeing her."

"Did he report it to the police?"

"He told them at the hospital that he fell on the pitchfork. People don't report things to the police where I live, you know? He's got a grow operation, too, so he wouldn't want any attention. If he'd called the police, they would've shut him down."

"How do you know this?"

"Alderpoint grapevine. The same goes for me."

I frowned. "The same?"

"I don't go to the police either. But Hannah's blackmailing me."

"How?"

"Well, it was my pitchfork. She gave it back to me and then told me I had to pay her five thousand dollars, or she'd go to the police. They'd get the DNA from the pitchfork, and I would go to jail for attempted murder."

Things weren't adding up. "I'm not suggesting you do this, but why didn't you just get rid of the pitchfork?"

"I washed it real good."

I thought for a minute, listening to the seagulls outside the window. "Okay, Ethan, this is clearly a matter for the police, despite your misgivings. We can go over to the courthouse together right now. The detective sergeant is a friend of mine, and I'm sure—"

"Yeah. I want to get this off my chest. Hannah's coming for the money tomorrow night."

I called Granville and gave her a quick summary. She had a few minutes free. I told our receptionist where I'd be, and because I didn't want to ruin the new car smell of my replacement Leaf, we walked.

Granville's office was on the third floor and had a view of the hills. She steepled her fingers while I related the story. When I was done, she asked Ethan to wait out in the hall. When the door closed, she said, "He's a nutcase, Garrett, is he not?"

"Could be." I told her about Ethan's roommate's attack on Jen.

She sighed. "Yeah, I don't know what to do about that bloody Alderpoint area."

"Murder Mountain," I said.

"Please don't call it that. We're getting a bad reputation as it is."

Actually, I planned to use that term as often as possible during the trial.

She stopped pacing and looked out the window. "Well, I've got a deputy who's itching to try out some new equipment. He'd love nothing better than to wire

Ethan up and see what the blackmailer says. If there really is one. Do you want in?"

"What do you mean?"

"Since you've been a good boy and brought this to the police, you deserve a biscuit."

I cocked my head. "A dog biscuit?"

Granville laughed. "I mean a cookie. If you want, you can go along and listen in."

"I could use a diversion. Any luck on my kidnappers?"

"You still won't tell me what they asked you to do?"

I shook my head. "Can't, sorry."

"Well, we think the nine-fingered man may be part of a group of growers out near Alderpoint. Does that jibe with what they demanded of you?"

I gave her my own version of Jen's inscrutable look. She asked me if I had indigestion.

We brought Ethan back in and explained the plan, then I went back to my office.

Chapter Fifteen

I WAS GETTING A little burned out by all the routine trial preparation work. As expected, Bella was dragging her feet on our discovery requests.

The fees for bodyguards were burning through our finances. Inspector Granville had been forced to reduce the patrols in my neighborhood. Twice, I'd had the feeling someone was following me, but both times it had turned out to be a false alarm.

In the afternoon, I received a call from RPPD.

"Mr. Goodlove, this is Deputy Waters. Detective Sergeant Granville said you wanted to listen in on our sting operation."

"For the blackmailing? Ethan Crowley?"

"Yes, sir."

Three hours later, I sat in the county's mobile command center one mile from the cabin Ethan shared with Sleepy Pete. Pete was out pursuing his hobby: lying in a drug-induced stupor in his car.

The command post looked like your standard Winnebago from the outside. I sat inside with Deputy

Waters, a new recruit who looked like he belonged in high school. He'd put on a little too much cheap aftershave. *Old Spice?* I'd expected walls bristling with state-of-the-art electronics, but much of the interior was empty. Humboldt didn't have the budget for sophisticated gear. Monitors displayed video from the three cameras installed in the two-room cabin. Ethan was wearing a wire, and several other mics around the main room acted as backups.

At the last minute, Ethan had seemed ready to back out, but I gave him a pep talk, telling him how good it would feel to be free of the blackmailing threats. I told him he was doing the right thing. Deputy Waters had instructed him on how to act, but I wasn't sure it had gotten through. Another deputy was hiding in the bushes nearby, ready to rush in if the meeting turned violent.

Eight thirty, the time for the appointment, came and went, but twenty minutes later Ethan jumped up. "She's here! She's h—"

"Damn." Waters slapped the counter in front of him. "The mic connection got loose when he jumped—no, it's back now."

The video was full color and high-def. Ms. Hannah Meese was late thirties with well-tended blondish hair that fell below her shoulders. She was a big woman in a white sundress printed with bamboo leaves. Her kindly face had wrinkles around her mouth and a small scar on her chin.

She embraced Ethan in a hug that knocked his hat to the floor. "Ethan, darling, how are you holding up?" After ending the hug, she picked up the hat and put it back on his head at a jaunty angle. "Should we get some tea?" Her voice was smooth, with a Midwestern accent.

"No, no," Ethan said. "I, uh, have some tea already made. Sit over here."

Hannah gave out a musical laugh. "Why are you so nervous, darling? It's just me."

They sat on a leather couch with rips in all the cushions, and she poured tea from the pot on the coffee table. "How's Pete doing?"

"I decided to give you the money." Ethan's voice had gone up an octave.

"Money?"

"The five thousand dollars."

She chuckled then got serious. "Whatever are you talking about, Ethan?"

Waters got up, "Damn it. She made us. Someone must have seen Reggie hiding or told her about the command center." He sat back down. "There, see? I think she's looking around for the cameras."

I wasn't so sure Deputy Waters was interpreting the situation correctly, but my duty to my client forced me to keep my mouth shut.

The next day, I convinced Ethan to have a talk with a friend of mine, a Dr. Quinton Lorenz, the head of the Sea View Sanitarium. The facility sat in the forest near Rio Dell, south of Redwood Point and far from the ocean. I'd always wondered whether the misleading name was confusing for the delusional patients.

Dr. Lorenz had generously carved out some time for Ethan and came out to greet us in his restful waiting room. Bald, with a salt-and-pepper beard, he wore a white cardigan sweater over a blue checked shirt. He greeted Ethan with a warm smile. Ethan looked back at me as he went into Lorenz's office, and I gave him an encouraging nod.

The good doctor winked at me. "It will take about an hour, Garrett," he said.

I set up my laptop away from the window. The peaceful environment wasn't having the desired effect on me because I'd once again had the feeling I was being followed. Jen and I shared a bodyguard, but he was with her. I phoned Inspector Granville, and she said she'd relay my concerns to the Rio Dell Police Department. Checking my email, I found that Bella had sent me the ballistics report on the bullet from Dean Shipley's head. I read the summary first. The bullet had been damaged, possibly ricocheting off something before entering Shipley's skull. As a result, the technician put the probability that the bullet came from Aksana's gun at only seventy percent. So, not a done deal.

Over the years, I'd learned that ballistics matching isn't as infallible as the public believes, and I was sure I could find an expert to reduce the seventy percent figure to something much lower. Luckily, I'd be spared that expense because the gun would not come up in the trial. I turned my attention to some motions and reviewed Jen's write-up on a character witness. I was so absorbed in the work that I jumped when Dr. Lorenz tapped me on the shoulder. He pulled a chair over and sat.

"Where's Ethan?" I asked.

"Ethan has decided to spend some time here getting treatment. He's given me his permission to discuss his case with you."

"There was no blackmail."

Lorenz nodded. "Quite right."

"Did he himself stick his neighbor with the pitchfork?"

"Indeed. Ethan suffers from severe PTSD. He desperately wanted to unburden himself, and you might say his subconscious developed this elaborate fiction, which allowed him to confess without admitting to himself what he'd done."

I rubbed my chin. "He was lying to himself."

"A lie that he thoroughly believed."

"Thanks for seeing him, Quinton. Do you think you'll be able to help him?"

"I'm hopeful," he said. "He's apparently never received treatment."

We both had to get back to work, but first we spent a few minutes talking about old times.

I said, "Remember the time that—"

Lorenz frowned. "What is it, Garrett?"

"That man out there. By the tree. I may be getting paranoid, but I've seen him before, and I think he might have followed me here. Do you recognize him? A patient, maybe?"

"I don't think so …"

As the two of us squinted trying to discern the man's features, his head exploded.

Chapter Sixteen

MINUTES LATER, A BRAVE—or perhaps foolhardy—physician ran out with his medical bag but stopped a few feet from the victim. There's not much you can do, I suppose, for someone whose head was in pieces.

I paced around Lorenz's waiting room as the police and sheriff's cars arrived. I occasionally looked out at the activity on the grounds. Soon, blue and red lights were flashing off the trunks of the trees in the forest. A deputy strung up crime scene tape.

The man's head had literally exploded, just like in the movies. Even at a distance, we'd seen the top of the skull fly up into the air.

I rubbed the back of my neck. *This was no coincidence.* And if that man had been following me, what did it mean? If he was with the kidnappers, he didn't want me on the case and he wanted Aksana put away—oh, crap.

I called Jen. "Is Aksana with you by any chance?"

"With me? No, why would she be with me?"

"I'll tell you later." I got the same response from Louella. I couldn't ask Granville whether Aksana's ankle monitor showed her anywhere near Rio Dell. Not without revealing my doubts about her. I'd find out soon enough.

Was there any chance Aksana was a hit woman? I'd considered that question before, but seeing her enemy's head explode gave the idea new life. Aksana had no motive for killing Shipley unless she'd been hired to do it. Murder for financial gain was a special circumstance in California, making it a capital offense.

Inspector Granville arrived two hours later. I watched her speak with the crime scene techs. They showed her something on the ground. She bent down and took a photo with her phone. Someone pointed my way, and she nodded and walked along the pathway toward the building.

I went to the doorway to the hall. When she appeared at the far end of the corridor, I waved. Dr. Lorenz had gone home. Apparently headshrinkers are upset by seeing heads explode. I didn't blame him.

Granville and I sat down in a waiting room that smelled of alcohol. She wore a shiny black shirt underneath a full-length leather coat. She leaned her cane against the wall. "Well, Garrett, I'm guessing you'll be seeing murder a little differently from now on. How do you like being on the front lines for a change?"

"Was it some kind of exploding bullet?"

"Apparently." She went over to the window. "You saw it happen?"

"Yes."

"It looks like the gun was fired from over there." She pointed. "Does that seem right, based on what you saw?"

"Ah, jeez, I guess so. I'll never get that image out of my head."

"Do you recognize this?" Granville took her phone from her pocket, made a few swipes, and turned it to me.

I took a breath and nodded. "That's him."

The photo was of a hand. A hand with the middle finger missing.

"Excellent. His name was Aaron Rodriguez. He was on our radar and suspected of being involved in your kidnapping. Nasty guy. A grower. He has two associates who will be headed to the nick. To jail. Certainly involved in your kidnapping. You can fire your bodyguards."

"Was he part of a Mexican cartel?"

She stood and picked up her cane. "Hard to say. They had a guerrilla operation going, up near Alderpoint."

"Guerrilla?"

"A grow on someone else's property. National forest land in this case. A real dog's dinner, with drugs, illegal pesticides, the full Monty. They had a lot to fear from whoever killed Shipley, which brings us to the question that's burning your lips."

"Question?"

She smiled. "Your babushka is in the clear. She's been puttering around in her home, according to her monitor."

I tried not to let my relief show.

* * *

About a week before the trial was to begin, Judge Stevens called us into chambers for a conference. I took an unobtrusive sniff of the air, trying to place the old-person smell. It was the same one as in my dad's nursing home. Talcum powder? Baby wipes?

Photos of her family covered every inch of the walls —if she got any more great-grandchildren, they'd have to appropriate another room for her. Many photographs were black-and-white, and I figured that some were snapshots of the judge as a young girl. I wandered around while waiting for Bella to arrive. "Quite a family," I commented.

I looked over to Judge Stevens, but she was absorbed with making notes on something or other, her tongue sticking out in concentration. Jen must have noticed, too; she winked at me.

My partner hadn't brought up our intimate night of snuggling. That was okay. She needed time. I'd been alone five years, but I sensed that an end was in sight.

Bella bustled in and with barely a glance in my direction sat down near Jen. My jaw almost dropped. She'd changed her hairstyle to some kind of pixie cut with the hair brushed forward—something you'd see on a teen who watched too much anime. Not a good look. I sat and attempted some small talk with her, but she only gave one-word answers and paged through her notebook.

Judge Stevens put away her project and cleared her throat several times. "Here is something I want to make very clear." She looked at each of us in turn. "There will be no mention of the gun in this trial. One slip of the tongue, willful or otherwise, and I'll declare a mistrial and slap you with contempt sanctions that will be outrageous. Is that clear?"

We nodded obediently.

She pulled her calendar toward her. "I've scheduled two days for jury selection, three days for the prosecution's case, and four days for the defense. Are we all on the same page?"

More obedient nodding.

She pulled her reading glasses down and stared at Bella. "Ms. Rivera, you've only appeared before me a few times. I have not been amused by your foot-dragging and your avalanching with the discovery materials."

"Avalanching" was a new term for me, but I knew what she meant. Both sides were required to submit lists of evidence and witnesses to the other side, and it was customary to bury nuggets of important data among an avalanche of useless information. It was a means of lying that attorneys used all the time. But Bella had taken the practice to extremes, and we'd had to hire an extra paralegal to sort through the material.

"And," Stevens continued, pointing her finger at Bella as though chiding one of her great-grandkids, "I have not appreciated your delay tactics either. The shenanigans end today, is that clear?"

Bella nodded. "Yes, Your Honor."

I liked the foot that we were getting off on.

Most lawyers believe that by probing for biases and researching demographics, one can seed a jury with citizens who are likely to be convinced by your arguments. But even if it were a one-sided affair, where you could go through the pool, picking out your ideal jurors like choosing dishes at a buffet, I didn't believe anyone could predict the thought processes of the complex human beings in the jury box. Once you add in the prosecution's effort to work against you, it's a game of chance. Like roulette rather than chess.

Jen disagrees. We've argued about this many times, and I always let her take charge of jury selection. Happy partner, happy practice.

There's no limit to how many jurors can be eliminated for cause. For example, if a prospective juror screamed that no one from a former communist state should be allowed to come into the US, we could probably get her struck for cause. The skill, according to Jen, came in eliminating jurors for no stated reason: peremptory challenges, of which we had ten.

Jury selection began on Halloween, and we'd soon seated a witch, a man dressed as a giant whoopee cushion, and a woman wearing a t-shirt that read, "Worst. Costume. Ever." Humboldt residents take the holiday seriously. Toward the end of the second day, we were out of peremptories, while Bella still had two left. Jen jiggled her legs and tapped her teeth with a finger when a young-looking man came up for his voir dire. Louella had flagged this guy as someone always trying, and failing, to make a quick buck. Jen felt this case was ripe for jury tampering and thought this fellow would be particularly susceptible to a bribe. I thought she was allowing her imagination to get away from her. Jen tried but failed to find cause for him to be struck, and the tattooed man was seated. Bella used her last peremptory challenge to eliminate a woman who looked so much like Aksana she could have been a relative.

At the end of the process, I was happy with the jury, but Jen was not. We had seven women and five men, with three jurors from the hinterlands of Murder Mountain.

Chapter Seventeen

ON THE FIRST DAY of the trial, Aksana didn't seem nervous. She was perhaps the most self-assured client I'd ever had. Even the three-month interval between the preliminary hearing and the start of the trial didn't seem to faze her. That kind of waiting period had most clients climbing the wall.

When Bella stood for her opening statement, I was struck by the similarity of builds between her and Aksana. But whereas my client came off as a stereotypically jolly fat person, Bella just seemed mean. Someone you wouldn't want to meet in a dark alley. I'm sure she'd intended her spiky haircut to give her a with-it appearance. Instead, she looked like a member of the Sex Pistols gone to seed.

"Ladies and gentlemen of the jury, thank you for your service," she said. "I know what an inconvenience it is to serve on a jury, but guess what? You guys lucked out. The verdict is so slam-dunk obvious that I'm surprised the case hasn't been dismissed."

Jen and I looked at one another. Bella had crossed the line of what is permissible during an opening statement. A lawyer may not state a personal opinion concerning the guilt or innocence of the accused. Objecting during an opening statement is frowned upon, however, and we decided to let it pass. Bella wasn't coming off as likable, so I didn't want to interrupt.

She glanced at me before continuing. "Mr. Dean Shipley was a simple farmer, and he didn't deserve to die. We will show that the defendant, Aksana Ivanova —" she paused and pointed to Aksana "—drove to his farm and murdered him. We have an eyewitness who saw Ms. Ivanova's car in the area and tire tread evidence that puts her near the farm. More importantly, she apparently cut herself while stalking him in the woods, and we will present a bloody rag that proves this. A bloody cloth from the farm. The DNA of the blood on that fabric matches the defendant's DNA. Not only that, but we'll present a hair that was found stuck to the cloth. That hair came from the head of the defendant."

Next, she pointed to me. "The defense will argue that the defendant has never been to Dean Shipley's farm, and they're going to present evidence that she was somewhere else when this gentle farmer was shot. But we'll show she had plenty of time to commit the murder. The defense will ask you, 'Why would this woman kill the farmer? What motive could she possibly have?' We don't need to prove motive for you to convict her, but we will show you evidence that Ms. Ivanova had a large amount of illegal cash soon after the murder, which she kept hidden. But it comes down to this: We know that even though she denies it, the defendant was at the farm when the murder was committed. And finally, ladies and gentlemen, we will show that Ms. Aksana Ivanova is not the gentle giant she claims to be."

My turn. I stood and walked to the lectern. I waited a few beats to build some suspense. I see trials as theater.

"Ladies and gentlemen, most of us live in a world governed by laws. Laws that are enforced by a dedicated police force. But up there on Murder Mountain, it's—"

Bella slapped the table and jumped up. "Objection! Prejudicial and inflammatory."

The outburst made Judge Stevens jump. She thought for a few seconds then cleared her throat. "Sustained."

I hadn't exactly planned for Bella to object, but I'd hoped she might. It portrayed her as unpleasant, harshly interrupting my gentle speech. More importantly, it allowed me to stress the lawless nature of that area of the state. Bella should have known I could find lots of ways to emphasize the "Murder Mountain" label without calling it that myself.

"Perhaps many of you have seen the Netflix documentary entitled *Murder Mountain*." I watched at least half the jurors nod. Despite being warned against independent research, I was sure that most of the others would Google it as soon as they got home. "It was an enlightening series about the area of our state that many call Murder Mountain. It sure opened my eyes. The area is so remote and so poorly served by the sheriff's department that it's almost like another country.

Another planet, even, where the inhabitants are on their own. Where they often take the law into their own hands. Because many are involved in illegal grow operations, is it any surprise they don't want to interact with law enforcement? It's the Wild West, where someone is more likely to settle a dispute with a six-gun than a call to nine-one-one."

I paused to let the image of gunfights in the streets sit in the jurors' minds. "We will show that there are plenty of bad hombres up there, probably including members of the Mexican cartel who have come north to take advantage of the high profitability of illegal marijuana cultivation. We will even present a witness who will show that when we visited the area, my partner was brutally attacked. Jen, will you please stand up?"

Jen stood. We were pushing the limits of what was allowed, but Bella stayed seated.

"Can you imagine anyone attacking this lovely woman?" I turned back to the jury and shook my head. "I tell you, that attack opened my eyes about that area of Humboldt. Thank you, Jen."

She sat.

"In such a rough world, anyone could have killed Mr. Shipley. In a lawless land like that, even a minor slight can lead to murder. It's an area, by the way, that leads the state in missing person reports. The prosecution wants to say that the bloody rag proves Aksana"—I pointed to her—"was at Mr. Shipley's farm, but in fact, it reveals something far more sinister."

The jurors had their eyes on me, eager for the story about to come.

I looked at them. "We will show that the bloody rag was planted in an effort to frame poor Aksana so that someone else could literally get away with murder. Whether it was the man who attacked my partner, a neighboring farmer with a border dispute against Shipley, or simply someone with a score to settle, someone else killed that man then stabbed Aksana at her home, collected her blood on a rag, and hooked that rag onto a strand of barbed wire on Mr. Shipley's property. We can prove this to you beyond any doubt."

I didn't want to overstay my welcome, but I had one more job.

"Let me tell you something about this wonderful woman, Ms. Aksana Ivanova. I'm amazed that her loving personality has survived the life she's led. Both her parents died young in her home country of Belarus, near Russia. It sounds incredible, but she actually worked in the salt mines for many years. In the salt mines. Her first husband died of radiation poisoning from the Chernobyl disaster. Her second husband was not a good man. He beat her, and only by changing her identity was she able to escape his abuse.

"I can say that if you knew Aksana the way Ms. Shek and I have come to know her, you'd never doubt her innocence. Thank you."

Bella started with evidence and testimony showing that Dean Shipley had indeed been murdered. The jurors seemed fascinated by the shark story and the x-rays of the bullet in the head. The bullet was admissible even though there would be no mention of a gun. At some point, the jurors would wonder about that, something that might work in our favor.

Next, Bella wanted to prove that Aksana had been at the scene of the crime even though she denied it.

Bella's voice filled the room. "The state calls Deputy Victoria Zinn."

Deputy Zinn, dressed in her uniform, was an unusually tall woman with pale skin and tight curls. After she was sworn in, she sat in the witness chair.

"Deputy Zinn, can you tell us about the afternoon you arrested Ms. Ivanova?"

The witness, in a melodious voice, described arresting Aksana at her house.

"Did you read Ms. Ivanova her rights?"

"Yes, I did."

"But she decided not to exercise her right to remain silent?"

Zinn laughed. "No, she was very friendly."

"Did she tell you she had never set foot on—"

I stood halfway up. "Objection. Leading."

"Sustained."

Bella glanced at me then back at the witness. "What did she tell you when you explained why she was being arrested?"

"I said she was under arrest for the murder of Dean Shipley, and she said she'd never been to that area. She'd never gone anywhere near it."

I gritted my teeth. I'd warned Aksana to say nothing if they arrested her, but like all clients, she ignored that advice. It was a perfect example of why people need to learn to keep their mouths shut and heed the Miranda warning. Had she said nothing, we could have suggested that she might have gone hiking there sometime in the past. Of course, that would have been a lie. Carly was right that lawyering often included deception.

"Did you mention where the murder had taken place?" Bella asked.

"No, I didn't."

"No further questions, Your Honor."

I stood. "Deputy Zinn, how long after the murder did you arrest Aksana?"

"Well, let's see. The murder was on July thirty-one, and I arrested her on September first, so about a month."

"Had the murder been in the news?"

"Yes, it had."

"Had the *Times Standard* printed a map of the farm in an article?"

"Oh, yeah. Okay, I see. Yes, I saw that."

"So, it wasn't surprising that at the time you arrested her, Aksana knew where the murder had taken place." Leading questions are allowed on cross-examination.

"No."

"No further questions."

Bella then called Zinn's partner, who confirmed both the Mirandizing and the statements that Aksana had made.

Next, Bella called Deputy James Lombard, the officer who had discovered the bloody rag at Shipley's. She placed People's Exhibit 1 into evidence. She went through the same questions we'd heard during the preliminary hearing.

I cross-examined him. "Deputy Lombard, you found the bloody cloth on what date?"

"September second."

"Were you involved in the search of the property soon after the murder was discovered?"

"No."

"And on that initial search, no one saw the cloth?"

"It is a big area."

"Please answer the question," I said.

"No, no one saw it."

"I'd think a rag like that would be hard to miss."

Bella stood. "Objection. Mr. Goodlove isn't testifying here."

Stevens said, "Sustained. Would you like to rephrase the question, Mr. Goodlove?"

"No, Your Honor. No further questions."

Bella popped up for redirect. "Deputy Lombard, Mr. Goodlove seems to be implying that someone couldn't have missed the cloth the first time they searched. Is that accurate?"

Lombard squirmed a bit. "It was a large area. Someone could have missed it. It was pretty hard to see."

"Thank you."

That was the opening I'd hoped for. "Permission to approach the witness, Your Honor."

Stevens nodded. "Okay."

"Deputy Lombard, this is a copy of your testimony from the preliminary hearing for Aksana." I took every opportunity to use her first name, personalizing her for the jury. "Could you read the highlighted line for me?"

"Uh. Yeah, 'Soon I saw a white cloth, like a handkerchief, stuck on some fencing. It was plain as day.'"

"'Plain as day.' No further questions."

Next, the prosecutor brought up Mr. York, the chief evidence technician for Humboldt County, a balding man with sleepy eyes. She went to the evidence cart and retrieved People's Exhibit 1, the bloody fabric found at the scene.

She handed him the plastic bag holding the evidence. "Can you tell us what this is?"

"Yes. This is the cloth found at the crime scene. It had blood on it as well as a single strand of hair."

"And did you have this blood and hair tested for DNA?"

"Yes, I did."

"And what did the results show?"

"The blood and hair belonged to the defendant."

"Thank you." Bella checked her notes. "And do you have an opinion as to how long it had been outside?"

"Not exactly, but I can tell you, after researching the temperatures and weather in that area of the county, the condition of the cloth was consistent with its having been outside for about a month."

Bella sat, and I stepped to the lectern. "Mr. York, could the rag have been outside for a month or more, yet the blood added to it more recently?"

"I don't understand."

"Oh, come on, Mr. York, it's not such a difficult question. Could the rag have been sitting outside for a while and then someone later put blood on it by, say, wiping a knife on the rag?"

Bella popped up. "Objection. Calls for speculation."

"Sustained."

"Would it be correct to say you know the rag was outside for a while, but you know nothing about the age of the blood?"

"Uh, yes. There's no way to know how old the blood sample is."

"You're sure of that?"

"Objection. Argumentative."

"I withdraw the question." I'd already given too many clues as to where I was headed. "Mr. York, I'm curious about the strand of hair. Can you tell me how long it is? I can give you your report if you wish."

"No, I remember. It is forty centimeters long."

"The hair is quite thin, isn't it?"

"Yes, but that's consistent with the hair of an older woman."

I glanced at the jury, putting on a puzzled frown. "I'm astonished that the hair remained attached to the fabric for a whole month. Isn't that surprising to you?"

York looked over at Bella then back at me. "Well, there was, uh, something that kept the two together."

I jerked my head back. "What? Was it stapled to the cloth? Duct taped? I don't understand."

He rubbed his balding head. "No, no. The hair passed through the cloth."

"*Through* the cloth? How could that be?"

He took in a breath and exhaled it through his nose. "Well, it … I'm not sure how it happened. It's just one of those … things."

"Things? I'm still not clear. The hair went through the material? In one side and out the other? I'm trying to picture it. Did you try pushing the hair, or some other piece of hair, into the cloth to make it pass through?" It was a compound question, but Bella didn't object.

The witness jerked his head up, perhaps wondering if I knew that he'd attempted exactly that. I was no mind reader; it was the obvious thing to do, and I'd tried it over and over without success.

"I may have tried that."

"And could you get the hair through?"

He hung his head. "I was able to with one sample, but not with hair as fine as the defendant's."

"Please speak up."

He repeated his answer.

"Okay, okay. I've got an idea. Perhaps someone put the hair through the eye of a needle, then passed the needle through the rag."

Bella stood and opened her mouth but sat back down without saying anything.

York said, "That's possible."

"Thank you, Mr. York. No further questions, Your Honor."

Following testimony tracing the incredible journey taken by Dean Shipley's head, Bella called Menachem Sitruk, Shipley's trusted assistant,.

Mr. Sitruk was not what you'd expect for an assistant to an illegal cannabis grower. He was born and raised on the island of Djerba in Tunisia, descended from a long line of Sephardic Jews who had immigrated to the island around the time of Columbus. He was in his early thirties, black, with close-cropped hair topped with a simple yarmulke. His eyeglasses sat on a wide nose, and his short, kinky beard was dotted here and there with gray.

Once he was seated in the witness box, Bella began her direct. "Thank you for coming today, Mr. Sitruk. I am sorry for your loss."

He gave a little bow.

"Tell me about your working relationship with Mr. Shipley."

"I have worked with Dean for fifteen years. He is— was—my boss, and I was his, well, his first mate, you might say." He had a strong accent but spoke impeccable English.

"What were your duties?"

"Although my expertise is in germination and breeding, I worked with him at all times. I managed the other workers."

"And where did you live at the time of his death?"

"I had a small house about a mile from the farm." Sitruk adjusted his wire-framed glasses.

"When did you last see Mr. Shipley?"

"As I've told the police, I said good night to him at eight p.m. on the evening of July thirty-first. Our work for the day was done, but Mr. Shipley liked to sit and contemplate his crops."

The usual methods of determining time of death don't work so well when the victim's head is discovered in the belly of a shark. Body temperature, stomach contents, rigor mortis— none of those were available. The death couldn't have occurred before the time he was last seen, of course, but the other end of the window wasn't so easily established.

"And when did you first notice that he was missing?" she asked.

"At six a.m. on the morning of August first. He always—"

"Thank you. Is that when you went to the farm to start working?"

"Yes. Always. That's when I realized that something must have happened to Dean."

"Is it a big farm?" she asked.

"Well, the property is large, yes, thirty acres, but the cultivated areas are smaller and spread out. As you know, it was an illegal operation, although we had planned to go legal next year. I had wanted to go legal this year. It was a source of disagreement between us."

"So the different patches of marijuana plants were hidden in the forest?"

I didn't object to the leading question.

"Yes, exactly right."

"You said you realized at six a.m. that Mr. Shipley was missing, but couldn't he have been somewhere else on the property?"

Sitruk shook his head. "We always met right outside his shed at six a.m. He was very regular in his habits."

"Is it possible that something happened? Maybe he heard a noise and went to investigate."

"Objection. Leading."

"Sustained."

"How can you be sure that he wasn't somewhere else on the property at six a.m.?"

"It was very quiet. If he'd been shot anywhere on the property, I would have heard it."

Bella turned to the judge. "Move to strike, Your Honor. Unresponsive."

"So stricken." Stevens instructed Sitruk not to elaborate.

"Permission to treat the witness as hostile." Bella wanted to put ideas in the jurors' heads with leading questions.

Stevens frowned. "Denied."

Bella kept trying to push the edge of the window past six a.m. The frustration showed in the muscles of her jaw. It was reasonable that Shipley was still alive at that time, and he had simply not been at the usual meeting place. Maybe he was sick, maybe a bear had chased him, maybe he had to minister to an ailing marijuana sprout. Maybe a friend had picked him up and taken him on a night of drinking, and he was passed out somewhere. Bella failed to get those points across.

"No further questions," she said.

I took the lectern. "If someone shot a gun on Mr. Shipley's property at, say, two in the morning, would you have heard it from your house?"

"No, I don't think so. Besides, there are often gunshots in that area."

"It's kind of a Wild West, outlaw environment?"

He nodded. "Yes, that's right."

"And you said it was quiet on the morning of August one."

"Objection. Repetitive."

"Sustained."

"How quiet was it on that morning?"

"Just the birds singing. The cicadas hadn't started their calls because it was still cool."

"Would you have heard a gunshot while you were on the property?"

"I think so, yes. We have booby traps—shotgun shells rigged to fishing line. We can always hear those."

As an example of how lawyers lie, I didn't ask whether he would have heard the shot if the gun had been equipped with a silencer. It was a lie of omission. It didn't bother me.

"Was Mr. Shipley's car present at the farm?" I asked.

"Yes, it was."

"And the farm is quite isolated. He wouldn't have been able to walk to town, for example. Is that right?"

Sitruk laughed. "No, that would not have been feasible."

"No further questions, Your Honor."

Chapter Eighteen

BACK IN THE OFFICE, Jen and I high-fived. We were well on our way toward discrediting the blood and hair evidence. If we convinced the jury it was planted, it would benefit us—further support that someone else was involved. Some outlaw willing to plant evidence. It was customary to move to dismiss the charges after the prosecution rested its case, and I was starting to think the motion might be granted.

Would Judge Stevens think about the gun at that point despite having ruled it inadmissible? Even judges could have trouble ignoring fruit of the poisonous tree if the fruit was especially juicy. That fruit was a lush peach that would make anyone salivate. But I was getting ahead of myself, and Jen reminded me of that. She suspected Bella had something up her sleeve. I did, too.

Jen asked me to sit in one of the visitor chairs in my office. She pulled the other one close so that our knees were almost touching. *What's going on?*

"Boss," she said, "I still think we need to hit Pete harder."

I jumped up. "Oh, no. Not that again. That's a dead horse. We—"

"So say you."

"Right. So says the boss." We were basing our case on a SODDI defense—Some Other Dude Did It. Jen felt our case would be stronger if we pointed specifically to Sleepy Pete as a suspect. A TODDI defense—This Other Dude Did It.

I walked to the window. "I still think it's—"

"No! It's not just because he attacked me. I don't blame him for that. He's had mental problems and was confused."

"But it's a lie," I said.

"It's not a lie. It may be misleading—"

"Same thing. We don't have any evidence or reason to believe he killed Shipley."

Jen crossed her arms. "Evidence, no. Reason, yes. He might have thought Shipley was Vietcong. It's reasonable. Maybe if Pete had had a gun when we were on our tour, he'd have shot me."

I hadn't thought of that before. The iconic photo of a Vietcong being executed in Saigon flashed into my head. I sighed. "Okay, maybe, but the man's been through enough. A murder investigation could send him over the edge."

"That makes little sense. First, he's already over the edge. Second, it sounds like you're saying that no one should be investigated for murder if they're unhappy."

"That's not what ... okay, how about we don't point the finger at him too strongly. We'll call Skye and have her testify about the attack, but just to show that there are other possibilities. Okay?"

"Fine."

"Fine."

Bella stood. "The People call Ms. Stephanie Cannon to the stand."

I paged through the witness list she had provided us, refreshing my memory. *Ah. Right.*

Jen looked at me with a questioning frown.

I leaned and whispered, "Neighbor. Said Aksana is gone a lot."

Except for expert witnesses, one side is not required to tell the other what a witness will testify about. They need only provide the witness's contact information so that the opposition can interview them. That's why avalanching is so effective. I'd been sure that Cannon was a chaff witness, a name provided to hide the witnesses they actually intended to call—the wheat. When I'd interviewed her briefly, she'd seemed unreasonably nervous. Sitting there waiting for her to appear, I decided I should have followed up on that.

"Ms. Cannon to the stand, please." Bella raised her voice, possibly thinking her witness was hard of hearing. She looked through the spectators as if playing Where's Waldo? A bailiff came into the courtroom, held his hands out palm up, and shook his head.

Bella turned to the judge. "May we have a short recess while we locate the witness? She was in the courthouse earlier."

Stevens nodded. "We'll take a fifteen minute recess."

While we waited, Jen and I decided that Cannon's testimony would be used to suggest that Aksana was not who she seemed.

"Aksana, you said you frequently go on trips, right?" I asked.

"Not many trips."

"And not out of the country."

"Right."

The search of her house had not turned up a passport.

All eyes turned to the back of the courtroom when a female bailiff came in, herding a nervous Stephanie Cannon in front of her. Cannon was sworn in and took her seat in the witness box. She was a middle-aged woman with naturally red hair and a bit too much eye makeup. Bella led her through the preliminaries, and the witness stated that she lived farther up Aksana's dirt road.

"You've told me that the defendant is often not home, is that correct?"

"Objection. Leading the witness."

"Sustained. Please rephrase your question, Ms. Rivera."

Bella nodded. "Have you noticed anything about Ms. Ivanova's house?"

"Yes. I work at night, and often, when I drive by her house, there are no lights on."

Biggus dealus. What was the point? My nervousness grew.

"Have you taken your dog on walks and been on the defendant's property?"

Cannon's eyes went to the door of the courtroom, suggesting to me she wanted out.

"Yes," she answered.

"Please tell us what you found when walking on the property in late August."

"Nothing important."

Bella said, "Please tell us, and we'll decide whether it's important. What did you find?"

"Nothing. Maybe I shouldn't have been there." She turned to Stevens. "Judge, I really don't want to do this."

Bella gripped the sides of the lectern until her knuckles turned white. I actually heard a little growl escape her.

"Your Honor," she said, "I would like to request that you declare Ms. Cannon a hostile witness." By doing that, Bella would be allowed to ask leading questions, which are otherwise prohibited on direct.

"Mr. Goodlove?"

"No objection."

"Granted. Ms. Cannon, you must answer the questions."

Bella asked, "In late August, while walking your dog, please tell us what you found on the defendant's property."

"Well, I didn't find it. My dog found it."

"And what was it?"

"Well, he started digging at the base of a big pine tree. He dug through the layer of needles, and when I got to him, I saw that he'd uncovered something."

"And what was that?"

"At first I thought it was a football. Potato, that's my dog's name, he pulled it out of the ground. It was too big to be a football, more like a basketball. All black. I picked it up, and I'm like, *Whoa*. It was squishy and covered in black duct tape."

"What did you do then?"

The witness bit her lip. "Well, I was curious, so I pulled back some tape. Inside were some plastic bags."

"And what was in those bags, Ms. Cannon?"

"Money."

I jumped up. "Approach, Your Honor?"

"Yes."

At the bench with Jen and Bella, I said, "Your Honor, this is the first we've heard of this."

Bella did only a fair job of hiding her smirk. "He had our witness list with plenty of opportunity to examine her."

"She said nothing about finding a ball of money."

Bella turned to me with a look of sneering disdain. "That's your—" She realized her mistake and turned to the judge. "That's Mr. Goodlove's problem. He apparently doesn't know how to interview an opposing witness. Do I need to hold his hand or something?"

Stevens rapped her gavel. "Don't … *squabble*. Mr. Goodlove, I don't see any violation of the rules of discovery."

"Your Honor," I said, "something stinks here. If Ms. Cannon reported to the prosecution that she'd found this ball of money, Ms. Rivera would have immediately requested a search warrant, and the sheriff would have executed it. That didn't happen."

Stevens turned to Bella. "Counselor?"

"It was only last night that I learned of Ms. Cannon's discovery. We met to go over her testimony, and she reluctantly disclosed to me what she'd found. We're preparing a search warrant now, but as you'll see if I may continue examining this witness, they probably won't find anything."

I scoffed. "Oh, come on."

The judge lived up to her nickname, Stormy Stevens. She stared at me like a cobra and hissed, "That's enough, Mr. Goodlove. I will not have that kind of … attitude in my courtroom."

"I just find it hard to believe—"

The judge slammed the gavel down. "I don't care what you believe, Mr. Goodlove. Unless you can come up with a valid objection, I will allow this testimony to continue. You are welcome to rebut it."

I glanced at the jury. They'd seen the judge direct her anger at me. Worse, I'd found in the past that once Stormy Stevens felt you'd crossed her, she was more likely to rule against you on wobbler issues for the rest of the trial.

When we'd returned to our places, Bella asked the witness, "How much money do you think was in—"

"Objection," I cried. "Calls for speculation."

"Overruled."

What! That was a clear error. It would not look good on appeal. Stevens seemed to send me a see-what-you-get-when-you-misbehave look, but I must have been imagining it. *That does it, she's senile.*

"Well," Cannon said, "the bill I saw was a hundred-dollar bill, and the bundle was about as big as a basketball." She held her hands out. "So—"

I stood. "Please, Your Honor. Same objection. This is crazy." I didn't want to bring any more attention to this bombshell, but I had to say something.

Stevens blinked a few times then instructed the jury to ignore the witness's answer and told Bella to rephrase her question.

Instead, Bella moved on. She'd made her point. "What did you do then?"

"Well, I thought about it. I'm an honest person, and I would never take any money that doesn't belong to me. I thought I would take it to the police or tell them where it was, but then I decided it was probably mob money."

I might have objected at that point, but I decided to let it go.

She continued, "And I didn't want the mob after me. So I put the corner of the tape back, and I buried it again in the same place. I brushed the pine needles over it so it wouldn't look like anyone had dug it up."

"And was that the end of it, or did you go back?"

Cannon shifted in her seat. "Well, I couldn't stop thinking about it. It kept me awake at night. So, about a week later, I went back, just to, like, confirm that I'd really seen it. I wasn't going to … well, I went back, and it was gone."

"Gone?"

"Yes. It was very clear where it had been, at the base of a big pine, and the ground had been disturbed. I told Potato to dig it up, but he wasn't interested. I poked around, but it was definitely gone. I wish I'd never seen it."

"Why is that?"

"Isn't it obvious? I'm sure it was mob money or from a drug dealer. That's why I changed my mind about testifying. But I didn't take any of it."

"No further questions."

Jen and I huddled. We considered moving on, but Jen thought she might get a point across, although it could be costly. She was the better choice for cross anyway, since she might seem more sympathetic, and I was apparently in Judge Stevens' doghouse.

Stevens cleared her throat. "Mr. Goodlove?"

"Sorry, Your Honor, we're ready now."

Jen stood and walked to the lectern. "Thank you very much for volunteering this information, Ms. Cannon. You were brave to come forward."

Cannon nodded.

"You live in a pretty isolated area, don't you?"

"Yes. Very."

"You implied you were worried the money might be connected to a mobster or a drug dealer, is that correct?"

"Yes."

"Do you have any reason to believe that there are people like that where you live?"

Cannon laughed. "You bet. Everybody knows that."

"What have you observed, for example?"

"Oh, I hear gunshots now and then. And cars drive by my house at all hours of the night."

"Ms. Cannon, if you were a mobster or a drug dealer hiding a bundle of money, wouldn't it be unwise, in case the police discovered the package, to hide it on your *own* property?"

Bella was up like a shot.

Judge Stevens rapped her gavel. "I know you know better than that, Ms. Shek. I should hold you in contempt." The judge stewed for a few seconds. "If there are any more shenanigans by you or Mr. Goodlove, I will fine you and maybe even remand you to jail." She turned to the jury. "You are to ignore Ms. Shek's question and anything that it may imply. The question will be stricken from the record. Court is adjourned for the day." *Rap!*

Jen's question was a blatant attempt to elicit speculation on a subject on which Ms. Cannon had no expertise, so Stevens was right to be angry. But, of course, Jen got our point across, and the jurors would have time to think about it overnight. Was that worth having the judge publicly chastise us? That was debatable. We would add a rebuttal expert witness to testify that drug money was often hidden on someone else's property and even on public lands, but I wanted to nip in the bud the idea of Aksana being paid cash for murder before it had a chance to flower in the fertile soil of the jurors' minds.

When we got back to the office, Aksana professed total ignorance of the ball o' cash. I was glad it hadn't come up in court that the bag was seen before Aksana was arrested and gone after she'd posted her bail. She'd paid a bail bondsman $100,000 for the million-dollar bail, so things fit together way too neatly. Bella dropped the ball on that one. Would she bring Cannon back to the stand?

The prosecution's next witness was the evidence technician who'd collected and analyzed tire tracks found near Shipley's farm. After laying the foundation for his testimony, Bella displayed, on the courtroom's plasma screens, a photo of tracks on one side and a test impression made with Aksana's tires on the other.

"And what does this show us?" she asked.

"It's an exact match," the technician replied. "The tire tracks were made by two-fifty-five, forty Z Goodyear Eagle Sport All-Season tires, the same ones on the defendant's car."

"I see. Based on your knowledge of the poorly maintained roads in that area, was there anything that struck you as odd about this tire?"

"It's not a truck tire."

Bella acted puzzled. "Why is that important?"

"Most people wouldn't drive in that area in the kind of car that would have those tires on it. They'd drive a truck."

"But apparently someone did, isn't that what you've shown us?"

"I'm thinking it was someone who wasn't aware of the quality of the roads there. Someone from—"

Jen stood. "Objection. Speculative. Move to strike."

I was sure Bella and the technician had planned that exchange.

"Sustained." The judge instructed the jury to ignore his last answer.

"No further questions, Your Honor." Bella sat.

Jen started the cross-examination. "Mr. Winston, did you find any distinctive marks on the treads that tied them to the exact tires on Aksana's car?"

"No, the tracks weren't fresh enough for that."

"No marks from, say, a nail in the tire?"

"No."

"How about a cut on a tread?"

"No."

"Thank you." Jen was particularly fetching in a formfitting gray blazer over a white tuxedo shirt. The matching skirt ended above her knees. "You said the tracks weren't fresh. Could you estimate their age?"

"Not exactly. They weren't more than about two months old."

"Two months? Wow. So, the tracks could have been made well before Dean Shipley died. Is that what you're telling me?"

Bella stood. "Objection. Asked and answered."

"Sustained."

"Mr. Winston, is the two-fifty-five, forty Z Goodyear Eagle Sport All-Season tire on Aksana's Toyota a relatively common model?" Jen recited the specs without even glancing at her notes.

"It depends on what you mean by relatively common. It sure wasn't common for those dirt roads."

She presented him with his notes. "Can you read the highlighted text for me?"

"Uh, 'My rough estimate for that exact model is that approximately one thousand cars in Humboldt County have that model.'"

"No further questions."

The testimony was damning, but we'd done what we could.

Chapter Nineteen

BELLA PRESENTED AN EYEWITNESS who claimed to have seen Aksana's Toyota Supra pass her home near Alderpoint in the middle of the night. She said she noticed the car because most vehicles in that area were trucks.

Jen took the cross and presented photos showing the woman's windows were dirty, trees stood between the house and the road, and even given that the spotlights on the woman's garage lit up the road, it probably would have been too dark for her to identify the car accurately.

It sounded good until the witness pointed to the photo of Aksana's car and finished her testimony with, "I don't give a hairy hoot about all that crapola. I know what I saw, and I saw that sports car drive by my house."

With the owner of a drugstore in Willits on the stand, the prosecution played the security cam footage of a self-check register. The large woman in the video wore a sun hat that obscured her face. Based on the credit card used in the transaction, that woman was Aksana. The video was dated July 15, 2019, sixteen days before Shipley died.

Bella froze the image. "Can you tell me what the defendant is holding in front of the scanner?"

"Yes. That's a Quikfone prepaid telephone. The kind used by drug dealers and other—"

"Move to strike, Your Honor," Jen said.

"Granted." Stevens turned to the witness. "Please just answer the questions."

Bella finished up, we had no questions, and the witness was excused.

Next up was Detective Sergeant Edith Granville. She wore a drab purple blazer with shoulder pads. Her royal, looking-down-her-nose demeanor was emphasized by the raised witness box, and she sat with her hands folded over the top of her cane.

Bella seemed like a lowly American after experiencing Edith's aristocratic bearing. "Detective Granville, were you able to determine the exact phone the defendant used?"

"Yes."

"How did you do that?"

"No other Quikfones were purchased from that store between July ten and July eighteen. Five minutes after the Quikfone was purchased, it was activated from the parking lot of the store."

"Did you get a warrant to examine the texts sent and received by that phone?"

"We did."

"And what did you find?" Bella asked.

"Only one text had been sent from that phone, on the morning of the first of August."

"And what did that text read?"

"Job compleet. The word 'complete' was spelled *C-O-M-P-L-E-E-T.*"

"It was misspelled," Bella said, "as a foreigner might misspell it."

I stood. "Objection. Leading. Prejudicial. Ms. Rivera is testifying. Many native speakers make spelling mistakes, especially when texting."

"Sustained." She turned to the jury. "Members of the jury, sometimes attorneys will ask questions they know are improper. Questions they know are not allowed. They ask them anyway, hoping that they'll make an impression on the jury. If I sustain an objection to a question, you must try to ignore what you heard, as though the question hadn't been asked."

Whoa! I'd never heard a judge say something like that to a jury and wasn't even sure it was allowed. In any case, it was a win for our side—diminishing the standing of the prosecutor. It came at a good time: in the midst of damaging testimony.

Bella recovered from the blow. "Was the text misspelled?"

"It was."

"You said it was sent on the morning of August one. Was that the day after Mr. Shipley was murdered?"

"Objection as to form," I said.

Stevens raised her thin eyebrows. "Form, Mr. Goodlove?"

"Compound question."

"I heard only one question."

"She was asking for confirmation of the date, and—"

"Overruled." She gave me a little glare, surmising correctly that I was trying to break up Bella's rhythm.

"I can't really answer that," Granville said.

Bella scratched her head. "Wasn't August first the day after the night of the murder?"

"We have only established that Mr. Shipley probably died sometime between July thirty-first at twenty-two-thirty and six o'clock on the morning of August first. You asked whether the text was sent on the day after the murder. I can't answer that."

Bella sat down. I hoped the jury was confused. I wasn't confused, and I prepared to plant the landmine that would sink the prosecution later on.

After taking my place at the lectern, I said, "It's good to see you Detective Granville. Thanks for coming in today."

"I really didn't have any choice, Mr. Goodlove."

I chuckled. "No, I suppose you didn't. I have only one question. What was the exact time of the text on this phone, which may or may not have belonged to Aksana?"

"It was sent at twelve fifty a.m. on the morning of August the first."

"I see. Thank you. I have no further questions."

"The People call Mr. Manny Sokolof."

Mr. Sokolof was a Russian martial arts instructor and looked it. He had a wide smile, and I wouldn't mind meeting him in a dark alley as long as we were on the same side. Especially if we had to fight someone mean. Like Bella.

His hair was like mine: a patch of hair in the middle of the top of his head and bald areas on either side. However, his hair was black and trimmed close to the scalp. His beard and mustache were the same. He wore an Under Armour compression shirt that showcased his muscles.

After he was sworn in, Bella asked, "Mr. Sokolof, are you familiar with the defendant, Ms. Ivanova?"

"Please call me Manny. No."

"I'm sorry. No?"

"Am not familiar with her. Met her one time. Very nice lady." His voice filled the courtroom, and the smile never left his face.

"Can you tell us wh—"

"She kicks my ass."

"She kicks your—"

"Kicked. When met her, she kicked my ass. Was big surprise." He laughed. "Very big."

"When you—"

"Not afraid to admit it."

Stevens leaned toward him. "Manny, please try to just answer the questions, okay?"

He gave her a thumbs-up. "You betcha. No problem."

"Mr. Sokolof," Bella said, "please tell us what happened when you first met Ms. Ivanova."

Jen nudged me, and I shook my head. I could have objected because the question called for a narrative answer. Lawyers are supposed to ask specific questions because long rambling answers don't give the opposing side the opportunity to object to individual questions that might introduce inappropriate responses. But I was sure the jury wanted to hear this larger-than-life, likable guy's story, and I didn't want to be the curmudgeon who took that away from them. I could make the objection later if necessary.

"I was giving demonstration of Sambo, you probably don't know what is." He wore a big smile.

Bella shook her head. "No, I don't."

"Sambo stands for *sozashchita bez oruzhiya*, which means 'self-defense without weapons,' okay? I am appearing at martial arts expo in San Francisco, on stage. I say Sambo is better than all others, like judo. I say, 'Does anyone want to fight me?' Lot of big deal guys there, and usually someone comes up on stage and we fight. Nobody raises hand, and I say, 'Is everyone a chicken?' Still nobody, okay? Then, I see Aksana get up. She is leaving, but I pretend she wants to fight, okay? I say, 'How about you, babushka?'"

He pronounced it with the accent on the first syllable —the Russian way, according to Aksana.

"So," he continued, "when I say this, 'How about you?' She calls out, *'Ya ne khochu delat' tebe bol'no,'* which means 'I don't want to hurt you.' Okay? I translate for audience and they laugh. To make long story short, she comes up. We put on helmets, but we are just making the jokes. She puts her scarf over her helmet, and that gets big laughs. Very funny. I smell alcohol, so I think she is drunk."

I was enjoying the narrative as much as everybody else in the courtroom.

"Then," he said, "I reach out to her, thinking maybe I hug her like lover to get more laughs. But then, big surprise, she does leg sweep. Holds one wrist, and very quick I am on my back on the mat. The audience goes crazy, like woo-woo-woo. Very fun. So, we start fighting more serious, but pulling punches, yes? I think, 'She could really hurt me.' With every move, she wins. Finally, she does what is called the 'calf crush.' Is like pretzel, hard to describe. But she puts my lower leg between her thigh and calf and pulls on her own ankle. Very effective. She is strong like bear. I yell uncle, and we get up. Hug. Crowd all standing and cheering. She walks away, waddling like old lady, and gets more laughings and cheerings. Very fun. She very nice lady. She is no murderer."

Bella raised her voice. "Move to strike the last sentence, Your Honor."

I stood, but Stevens waved me down. "On what grounds, Ms. Rivera?"

"Unresponsive. Speculation. Lack of personal—"

"Denied. You invite a narrative answer, you live with the results."

Bella took a few seconds to compose herself and looked up from her notes. "I understand, Mr. Sokolof, that you have a video of this?"

"Yes."

I half expected the jury to jump up and cheer. The tattooed juror in the back row, the one we were worried about, pumped his fist in a "Yes!" gesture. I'm sure they were thinking, *Maybe jury duty isn't boring after all.* I could have found a way to object to the video and have it excluded, but that would make me the bad guy in the eyes of the jury. Besides, I wanted them to see it.

The video matched Manny's narrative well and was even more exciting. I cherished the way it showed Aksana's sense of humor. Everyone in that audience loved her and wanted to take her home to dinner. I saw that same love on the jurors' faces. We'd previewed the video, and I'd hoped for that result. It showcased Manny's obvious affection for our client. I made a note to emphasize at some point that Shipley wasn't killed with some kind of Sambo move.

Bella sat down. *Does she realize what a disaster the testimony was?*

At the lectern, I said, "I really enjoyed that, Manny. Thanks."

He laughed and nodded. "Was fun."

"Manny, are you a criminal?"

"Am I criminal? I know you just make the joke, but no, I am not criminal."

"You're not a drug dealer?"

"No."

"You're good at fighting, but you're not an international hit man, are you?"

"No. I am good man. Responsible. I tell my students, 'Sambo is for self-defense.' If student is mean? Wants to really hurt people? That is no good. I tell him, 'No. I don't want you in my class. You go away.'"

"Have you seen Aksana since that day? Until today?"

"No. I try to find her. Russian friend see her picture in article about murder, tell me, I call police here to find her, and that's why I am here now. I am good judge of people. I know right away, she is good person."

"She didn't strike you as a murderer, did she?"

He boomed out his answer. "No."

"Objection! Relevance, speculation, improper character, improper opinion, lack of foundation. Move to strike."

"Sustained." Judge Stevens made a gesture that I would have thought way too modern for her. She poked two fingers toward her own eyes then at mine: *I'm watching you.*

"No further questions."

On the way out, before the bailiff could stop him, Manny leaned over the defense table and hugged Aksana awkwardly. When he left, there were tears in her eyes.

Had I been the prosecutor, I'd have sold my grandmother to find something to follow that, but either Bella didn't understand the impact of the testimony or she didn't have anyone else.

"The prosecution rests," she said.

Jen invited me to an early dinner at Masaki's, a Mongolian grill—the kind where you fill a bowl with meat and other ingredients, and a chef pushes them around on an insanely hot griddle then gives them back to you. She knew it was my favorite restaurant.

There were only two other couples there, but the place already had the steamy scents of teriyaki, garlic, and chicken. The cooks were laughing about something and speaking rapidly in some Asian language.

I put some thinly sliced chicken into my bowl and leaned down to Jen. "Is that Chinese?"

She nodded. "Wu dialect."

"What are they talking about?"

She smiled and added broccoli to her bowl.

"What?"

"You. And me."

181

I watched them. Neither was looking directly at us. "What are they saying?"

"You're not going to like it."

"C'mon."

"One said that the big ... *gwailou* ... which means 'Westerner'—"

"Derogatory?"

"Not really. He said you are ... *lao niu chi nen cao*. An old cow eating tender grass."

"So, uh, robbing the cradle."

"You got it."

I laughed. "Fair enough." I was okay with it. Fifteen years separated us. I wasn't a sleazeball. I could look myself in the mirror ... but it helped to ignore my wrinkles.

We drank beer while my critics cooked.

Jen wasn't as happy as I was with the progress of the trial.

"But consider this," I said, "we're off the character-witness hook." Prosecutors rarely call a witness to disparage a defendant, because the rules of evidence don't allow them to posit that someone committed a crime because of his or her character. However, if we brought witnesses to testify that Aksana was a wonderful human being, the prosecution could then call rebuttal witnesses, and that rarely goes well. So, Manny was a gift.

One of the cooks brought over our food, and I thanked him.

Jen took a delicate bite of broccoli. "Okay, so Massive Manny likes Aksana after tussling with her a few minutes. How does that help? Our sweet old lady has been transformed into someone who could kill with her bare hands. Literally. The jury will wonder where she learned how to fight. Who knows, maybe they'll figure she killed Shipley with a leg sweep and a calf crush."

"I thought of that, but the jury knows he was shot. They saw the bullet in the x-ray."

"Still, the image of a decrepit old babushka in the potato fields is out the window. She even showed, in the video, how good she is at pretending to be frail—when she walked off the stage."

I stabbed a piece of pork with my chopsticks. The food was outstanding. "I still think we came out ahead. 'Sure, those Russkies are rough-and-tumble, but that Aksana, boy, she has a heart of gold.'"

After we ate in silence for a while, I said, "I'm still bothered by why the bad guys framed Aksana instead of killing her. They could have killed her at her house instead of getting hair and blood for setting her up."

Jen finished her bite. "I agree, but maybe they *were* trying to kill her. Her pile driver punch and Louella's appearance foiled that, so they settled for using the blood on the knife."

"Maybe." I thought for a while. "I still haven't decided on the order of our witnesses. What do you think?"

"One, discredit the blood evidence. That's so obvious we'll have the jury eating out of our hands and Bella running with her tail between her legs."

"Maybe she really does have a tail."

Jen gave me a dirty look. "Two, we show that everyone on Murder Mountain goes around shooting their neighbors if they get slightly peeved at them."

"Check."

"Three, we present the Petaluma security cam footage that puts her hours away from Shipley's."

"That's the key. Only one problem."

"What's that, boss?"

"We don't see her face. Worse, I'm not convinced she's innocent. If I'm not convinced, what will the jury think?"

"They'll think what we tell them to think."

"I'm not as confident as you are."

The bigger of the two cooks brought our check to the table, and Jen said something in rapid-fire Chinese. The cook's face reddened. He put his hand to his mouth and walked away.

"What did you say?"

"I said, '*Jing shui bu fan he shui.*'"

"Which means?"

She shrugged. "The meaning gets lost in translation. Literally, it translates to 'Well water does not intrude into river water,' which means—"

"No, don't tell me." I sipped my beer and looked at the ceiling. After a while, I shook my head. "No, I give up. What does it mean?"

"It means '*Mind your own business.*'"

Chapter Twenty

OUR FIRST WITNESS WAS an expert on blood evidence. Dr. Sednov didn't come cheap, but I was confident that he'd be worth every penny of Aksana's money. I'd have preferred a little more gray in the temples, but he looked like a scientist with his heavy-framed glasses and trim beard. It was easy to picture him in a lab coat.

I'd only gotten through a part of his résumé when Bella stipulated to his expertise in the field of blood, hair, tissue, and other biological samples.

"Doctor," I said, "I understand that your lab is working on an interesting new area of forensic blood analysis that's particularly relevant to this case."

"That's correct."

"And what is that?"

"We have developed a technique to analyze the age of blood samples. Blood is the most common bodily fluid found at crime scenes, and our new procedure lets us determine the TSD with a great degree of accuracy."

"TSD?"

He laughed. "Sorry, one gets so used to talking in jargon. TSD means 'Time Since Deposition.' As bloodstains age, natural chemical processes occur that can be analyzed with Raman spectroscopy. We can nondestructively measure those changes and tell how old a bloodstain is."

"Like one year, ten years, twenty years?"

"Oh, no. More like one hour, one day, one week, and so on up to two years. We hope to eventually have a handheld device available that will give police instant readouts in the field. It's revolutionary."

"Interesting," I said. "To summarize, you've developed a new tool that police can use to figure out how old a bloodstain is." There's a fine line between making sure jurors understand and boring them. I hoped my summary would counteract the effects of the jargon.

"Yes, that's right."

"May I approach the witness, Your Honor?"

"You may," Stevens said.

I took an exhibit from the cart. "This is People's Exhibit one. Is this the blood sample I had you analyze?"

"It is."

"What can you tell us about the age of the blood on this rag?"

An experienced witness, he turned to the judge. "May I consult my notes?"

"You may."

"Let's see … we examined this stain on sixteen September and determined that it was between fourteen and nineteen days old."

"I see. So, checking my calendar, it was deposited sometime after August twenty-seventh." I paused. "How much of a margin of error would there be in that?" I asked.

"A few days."

"Could that blood have been deposited on July thirty-first of this year?"

"No. Absolutely not. It would get technical, but I could show how that would be absolutely impossible."

"Thank you, I'll take your word for it. Now, did you find out anything else interesting about the blood sample?"

"I did. We found oil in the sample, which we determined was a product called Rem Oil, put out by Remington."

"And what is that?"

"It's essentially a gun oil. It includes Teflon, and it's used to lubricate guns and knives."

I put on a puzzled frown. "Why would someone want to lubricate a knife?"

"Sorry. It also protects metals from corrosion."

"So, would what you saw on that rag be consistent with someone being stabbed with a well-oiled knife on or around August thirty-first and then having the blood wiped on that rag?"

"Yes. And in fact, the pattern of blood is consistent with someone wrapping the cloth around a knife and pulling the knife down."

I glanced at the jurors. A few had glazed-over eyes, and an older woman in the back row might have been drifting off. I was getting bored myself. I clapped my hands. "Okay, let's move on to this business of the hair sample."

He'd seen photographs of how the hair passed through the cloth. He'd done experiments with strands of Aksana's hair that I'd sent him and similar pieces of fabric.

I ended by asking, "How could that hair have gotten through the cloth like that?"

"The only way would be to put the hair through the eye of a needle, pass the needle through the cloth, then slide the needle off."

"Couldn't it have happened any other way?"

"Extremely unlikely."

"No further questions."

Bella was slow to rise. She had to do something to save her case.

"Dr. Sednov, you've told us this blood-dating technique is new, is that right?" she asked.

"It is."

"So, it's not a proven technique like, say, fingerprinting."

"It hasn't been around for many years, if that's what you're saying, but the technique has been put to the test in several labs here and one in Germany."

"But no police departments use it routinely, is that correct?"

"Yes, but—"

"Thank you."

She sat. I stood.

"Dr. Sednov, why don't police departments use it routinely?"

"Well, first, they don't know about it, but second, we haven't made it available. We don't have the capacity to handle a lot of requests. That will change after we develop the portable unit."

After a short break, Jen called Louella to the stand. We'd made the case that the blood was deposited on the rag not on July 31, but toward the end of August. Next, we'd show how and exactly when the blood got there.

I often wished the trial system worked a little differently. Well, a lot differently. Specifically, I wished I could turn to the jury and ask, "Okay, are you all convinced that the bloody rag was planted? I can give you more evidence, but if you're all convinced … show of hands? … You are? Okay, thanks." But since it didn't work that way, I often needed to drive home a point, even if some jurors rolled their eyes.

Louella was excellent on the stand. She'd testified many times when she was with the police department as well as afterwards as a private detective. We'd gone over her testimony ahead of time, but it was hardly necessary. We needed only show that an unlicensed phlebotomist had collected a blood sample from Aksana in an unconventional manner.

After the preliminaries, Jen said, "Please describe the assault."

"I was driving toward the house and saw Aksana clearing dishes off the table on the deck. Something flew out of the bushes. At first I thought it was a bear. A knife flashed in my headlights, so then I knew it was a person. He was dressed in black, with a black balaclava over his head. It might have been a ski hat with eye cutouts."

Louella looked at the jurors as she spoke. "As I watched, he yanked Aksana's head back by her hair and sliced the knife into her body. I accelerated up the lawn, drew my pistol, and fired a shot into the air. Aksana hit the man, knocking him down. By the time I got out of my car, he'd fled back into the forest. The whole episode took only seconds."

"Was Aksana injured?"

"Yes, she had a long, slicing cut along her upper arm. Very deep. It must have been painful."

"Was there a lot of blood?"

Louella nodded. "Yes. The blood dripped down her arm and onto the deck. I applied a tourniquet."

"What did you do next?"

"I called for the police and an ambulance. Then we bandaged up her cut."

"Did the police and ambulance arrive quickly?"

"No, it was at least an hour and a half."

"An hour and a half?" Jen put some mild shock into her voice. "That long?"

"The area is far from the closest sheriff's station and even farther from any hospital."

"No further questions."

Bella took the lectern. "We've heard testimony that the defendant is some kind of expert at martial arts."

Louella said nothing.

"Was that evident when the person attacked her?"

"She hit him very hard. He fell onto the deck. Then he scrambled up and ran away."

"Thank you." Bella sat.

On the way out, Louella leaned over to me and whispered, "I need to talk to you about the jury."

Next, I brought my doctor to the stand. I'd called her after the assault and asked her to meet Aksana at the ER.

Dr. Vishneya is young looking, but she has an exhaustive knowledge of medicine.

"Has Ms. Ivanova given you permission to discuss her medical information?"

"She has." Vishneya had a wonderful lilting Indian accent.

"Please tell us what you found when you examined her."

"Ms. Ivanova had a deep laceration extending from just below the shoulder almost to the elbow. The cut nicked the anterior humeral circumflex artery."

"Did that cause a lot of bleeding?"

"It certainly would have. Bleeding was under control by the time I saw her."

"Could you tell how old the cut was?"

She cocked her head. "I don't understand."

"Could the cut have been made, say, a month earlier?"

"No, no, no. Of course not. It was a few hours old."

"What was Ms. Ivanova's demeanor?"

The doctor laughed. "She was joking around. She said something about how she wished it was the bear that had gotten into her garbage, because then she would have given it a thrashing. Some people are naturally happy. I liked her immediately."

Dr. V. has treated me for depression. I guess I'm not naturally happy.

"Did you examine Aksana again the next day?"

"I did, at your request. You asked that I look for other wounds on her body. Head to toe. I did a thorough exam."

"Were there any other significant cuts on her body?"

"No."

"Any cuts that might have been made a month earlier?" I asked.

"Most minor cuts heal within a few weeks, so I couldn't say. Ms. Ivanova has diabetes, so healing would take a little longer, but still, I wouldn't see them."

"May I approach the witness, Your Honor?"

"Yes."

I picked up People's Exhibit 1 and took it to the good doctor. "This cloth has Ms. Ivanova's blood on it. Could a laceration big enough to produce this much blood have healed enough that you saw no evidence of it a month later?"

She examined the evidence through the plastic bag, manipulating it so that the full rag was visible. "No, I don't think so. I would have seen a scar."

"How about if it was a small cut, small enough to disappear by the time you examined her, but she held this cloth against the cut and the blood accumulated?"

"No. In that case, the blood would have clotted before this much blood could've been deposited."

"No further questions."

Bella said, "No questions, Your Honor."

Out in the hall, Bella cornered Jen and me. "Voluntary manslaughter. Three years in the state pen." Bella's first plea offer.

I smiled. "She won't take it. Someone's trying to frame her for something she didn't do, and that's obvious to the jury."

Bella must have been on a diet because she was looking thinner. Another thirty pounds and lose the pugilistic attitude, and maybe she'd be kind of attractive.

"Here's the thing, Garrett," she said. "You and I both know she did it, and if it weren't for that numbskull CHP officer, she'd be in prison now, maybe on death row. We have information that she is indeed a hit man— hit woman."

"Then why didn't you go for special circumstances?"

"We didn't have enough to prove murder for hire. You're an honorable man, Garrett. I've always been impressed with you. Think about what it would mean to let a hit woman go free. How will you feel if she kills again?"

I squinted. "Aksana isn't a hit woman. It sounds like you're asking me to go against the best interests of my client."

"Not at all. I'm simply giving you a reason to see that manslaughter would be a good compromise. Maybe you could convince her to take the deal."

"She'd be out in a few years," I said.

Bella shrugged. "Maybe if she were in prison for a while, she'd decide to give up her evil ways."

Or they'd find out more about her and charge her with other crimes.

"By the way," Jen said, "she found that gun on the side of the highway where Shipley's killer threw it out the window. Don't forget that."

Bella scoffed. "Right. Present the offer to your client. God knows she'll be able to take care of herself in prison. She might even enjoy the fighting."

I later presented the plea deal to Aksana, but she just laughed. In fact, the whole trial almost seemed like a casual amusement to her. Did that argue that she was innocent? No. I'd had some innocent clients, and they were even more nervous than the guilty ones.

Over the lunch break, Louella met us in our office.

"You know you smell like a fruit stand, right?" I leaned forward and sniffed. "What's the vape of the month? I'm guessing strawberry ... strawberry banana?"

She said, "*Jing shui* ... blah bl blah blah."

Jen laughed.

"*What?*" I looked from one to the other.

Louella said, "Chinese for 'mind your own business.' Something about pissing in the well. So, I want—"

"You report on our dates or something?" I asked Jen. "You two discussed our dinner at Masaki's?"

Jen smiled. "She employs her investigative skills to worm things out of me."

I sat back. "Oh, I get it."

"What?" Jen said.

I shook my head. "I didn't think it worked that way."

Louella slid her reading glasses down her nose and looked at me.

"That Olympic cyclist was a gossip at heart, so now —"

"Yeah, that must be it." Louella said, deadpan, but I caught a brief smile. "So, I have some news about the jury. I think there's some tampering going on. Someone on the jury is getting paid."

"Huh," I said.

Jen scratched her chin. "Which way?"

"It doesn't matter which way." I leaned forward. "We need to take this to the judge."

"Hold on." Louella held up a hand. "This is only rumor and scuttlebutt. And I don't know which way. Plus there was something I saw."

"What?" I asked.

"I was at Starbucks on Fifth, and I saw the tattooed juror get out of a limousine."

I picked up a pen and tapped my cheek with it. "Not enough to go to the judge with."

"You don't think so?" Jen said.

"It would be a mess. There's nothing illegal about getting out of a limousine, and it would open us up to the suspicion that we were watching the juror, which we were not. It could result in a mistrial, but I suspect that even if we brought it to Stevens' attention, she'd just say there wasn't enough to go on. She'll think we're trying to get rid of a juror we don't like."

Chapter Twenty-One

I STOOD. "THE DEFENSE calls Skye Maritz."

I'd called several witnesses to demonstrate the lawlessness of the Alderpoint area. I decided to end with Skye, the woman who'd given Jen and me a tour of Murder Mountain. She held her hemp fedora in one hand as she took the oath, and her smile lit up the courtroom. She once again wore a tie-dye dress, but this one was more formal, with a paisley pattern and considerably more cleavage showing.

"Thank you for coming, Ms. Maritz, and thank you for the tour you gave us of the Alderpoint area."

She announced, "We have affordable cannabis tours for everyone, even lawyers."

The jurors and spectators laughed. Nice way to get her plug in.

"Are there a lot of police in the Alderpoint area?"

She laughed. "Not at all. The closest sheriff's station is in Garberville, and it's often deserted."

There were eight Google reviews for that station. All had one star, with comments like "Worthless." One reviewer wrote, "Watch Murder Mountain on Netflix."

"How long does it take a deputy to respond when someone in that area calls nine-one-one?"

She smiled. "They don't. People rarely bother calling nine-one-one."

"Why not?"

"They take care of things themselves."

I tilted my head. "What do you mean?"

"Let's say a neighbor dumps something on your property. Calling the police wouldn't accomplish anything. So, you either go talk to the guy, maybe with your gun at your hip, or you get your friends together."

"It sounds like—"

"Plus, people don't like the police."

"Why not?"

"Well, most of them are involved somehow in illegal grow operations. If the police came, they'd notice what's going on and might come back later with a search warrant."

"Do you know much about growing marijuana?" I asked.

"About as much as there is to know. I don't do it any longer, but I worked on some grows for many years."

"Most of it is a cash business, is that right?"

"One hundred percent cash," she said, "for the illegal farmers, at least."

"And there's a lot of money involved, right?"

"Of course. Tens of thousands of dollars. More."

"Let's say a grower gets a payment of, say, eighty thousand for a harvest. What does he do? He can't take it to the bank, is that right?" I asked.

She laughed. "It's a huge problem. All successful growers have a problem of too much money rather than not enough."

"So do they hide it under a mattress?"

"Some. But if the cops got a search warrant, they'd be screwed. They usually bury it somewhere."

"In their backyard?"

"Ha! No, the police would find that. They usually bury it far away. There are a lot of stories of growers forgetting where they hid it. Like squirrels burying nuts."

"Wait …" I turned slightly and frowned, letting the jury see my Oscar-worthy acting. "They bury it on someone *else's* property?"

"Sure, why not?"

"Wouldn't they worry that someone else would find it and keep it?"

"That risk is lower than that the cops find it and you go to jail for years. If you're taking in a million a year, you can stand to lose a hundred thou now and then."

I looked over my notes, letting that sink in. Also, I wanted a divider between that and my next topic.

"Ms. Maritz, something a little scary happened on our tour. Can you tell us about that?"

She frowned. "The tours are one hundred percent safe. I don't know what you mean."

"I'm talking about the encounter between my partner, Jen Shek, and a man known as Sleepy Pete."

Skye crossed her arms. "I don't really remember that."

I didn't expect that. "May I approach the bench, Your Honor?"

She gave her permission, and Bella, Jen, and I walked to the bench. I said, "Jen was attacked by a friend of Ms. Maritz. She'd like to protect him. May I treat her as a hostile witness?"

"Any objections, Ms. Rivera?"

"No."

"Okay, Mr. Goodlove, permission granted."

Back at the lectern I asked, "Ms. Maritz, didn't Sleepy Pete attack my partner?"

"Sleepy Pete suffers from PTSD, he wouldn't hurt a fly."

"Move to strike as unresponsive, Your Honor. Please instruct the witness."

"So stricken." Stevens turned to Skye. "Ms. Maritz you must answer Mr. Goodlove's questions directly and honestly. You are under oath."

Skye's wide smile was gone.

I asked her, "Ms. Maritz, did Sleepy Pete attack my partner?"

"He was confused ... yes he did."

"What happened?"

"Sleepy Pete ... uh ... tackled Ms. Shek and held her down on the ground. You came running and jumped and pulled him off your partner and hit him."

"And what did you do at that point?"

"I didn't want you to keep hitting him. He's frail. A Vietnam vet. I don't want him to get into any trouble. He's harmless. He just gets confused."

"So what did you do?"

"I took out my revolver and shot into the air," she said. "Once or twice. To get your attention."

"Do you always carry a pistol, Ms. Maritz?"

She crossed her arms. "It's a good idea in that area."

"Because it's kind of like the lawless Wild West?"

"Yeah, I guess so."

"No further questions."

Bella got Maritz to say that many of the people in the area were nice and peaceful. Salt of the earth, she said. But Bella's heart wasn't in it, and she recognized the danger of eliciting further testimony that could hurt her case.

She sat down.

Our next piece of evidence, we hoped, would give Aksana an ironclad alibi.

On the stand was Glen Craw, the owner of a twenty-four-hour fast-food joint, the Burger Pit, in Petaluma. After getting permission to approach the witness, I handed him Defense Exhibit 6, a receipt taken from one of the fast-food bags in the back seat of Aksana's car.

"Mr. Craw, do you recognize that receipt?"

"Well, not this exact one, but it is a receipt from my restaurant." Mr. Craw was short enough that I wondered whether he had some kind of growth hormone problem. He was bald with a comb-over that wasn't fooling anyone.

"Can you read the date and time on the receipt?"

He pulled reading glasses from his pocket and put them on. "Let's see. August one, 2019, two-oh-three-oh-seven a.m."

"Thank you. That means that whoever got that receipt purchased something at around two a.m. on August first, is that right?"

He shrugged. "A grilled fish burger."

"Yes. I would now like to play the security camera footage from your restaurant for two a.m. on that day." We'd already gone through the steps of laying the foundation for the video. Bella had objected, but it was admitted under the work product exception to the hearsay rule.

Long gone were the days when establishments kept only a day's worth of recordings on a set of rotating tapes. Mr. Craw had supplied a week of video on both sides of the night of the crime.

The video appeared on the plasma screens, the date and time stamp rolling at the top left. It was in color and high-def. In came Aksana wearing the same sun hat she often wore over her scarf. Every time I watched the video I willed her to look up or remove the hat, but of course it never happened. It would have been nice to see her face, but it wasn't necessary. She had the same shape and distinctive waddle as she approached the register. I'd made sure that she was wearing the same brightly colored dress as the one in the video.

"Stop it there, please."

The video stopped with a good view of Aksana.

"Do you see the person at the register in this courtroom?"

Craw nodded. "Yes. It's that woman, there."

"May the record show that Mr. Craw pointed to the defendant, Aksana Ivanova."

I let that sink in for a moment then directed that the video be set to a point I'd given the technician in advance.

"Can you tell me what's happening here, Mr. Craw?"

"Well, she's put her credit card into the reader."

"Yes. Does that show on the receipt?"

"It does. She paid with a Mastercard."

"Yes, thank you. Let's watch the rest of the tape." The records we subpoenaed from Mastercard confirmed that the fish sandwich was purchased with Aksana's card. I would present that later.

After paying, Aksana stood waiting for her food. She was the only customer. She must have been tired from driving because she put her arms up above her and put one hand against the wall beside the counter. It struck me as odd, and when I'd asked her about it, she said her shoulder was sore. She said her doctor had recommended that stretch. The food arrived, Aksana took it, turned, and waddled out.

Something about the video was tickling the back of my mind. *What was it?*

"Mr. Goodlove," Stevens said, "wake up!"

"Sorry, Your Honor. No further questions."

Bella walked to the lectern. "Mr. Craw, do you remember seeing the defendant come into your restaurant?"

"What? No, I wasn't there. I only work during the day."

"Her face didn't appear in the video. Are you an expert at recognizing people from their body shapes?"

Mr. Craw was getting nervous, as if he were on trial. "I don't know what you mean."

"Well, you're saying you recognize the defendant in this video when we can't even see her face, how could you possibly know that—"

I said, "Objection. Argumentative."

"Sustained."

Bella took a breath. "Do you see a lot of women in your restaurant who are overweight or obese, like me, for instance?"

"Yes. We have an obesity crisis in this country. It's not my fault. I serve salads."

I laughed and so did a lot of others in the courtroom.

"Mr. Craw, do you think it's possible that the woman in that video is just someone whose body looks like the body of the defendant?"

"She's wearing the same dress." He pointed.

"Can't two different people own the same dress?"

"Yeah, I guess."

"You guess?" Bella sneered. "Can't two women own the same dress?"

"Objection. Argumentative."

"Overruled."

Craw said. "I guess—I mean, yes, they can."

"Does it surprise you that this woman was wearing a sun hat in the middle of the night?"

He shrugged. "Not really. I've seen a lot of strange clothing."

After a pause Bella said, "Thank you for driving up here from Petaluma today. Do you remember how long it took you?"

"I had to come. It took me—let's see, I left this morning at—it took me four hours."

"Four hours exactly?"

"Pretty near. From the restaurant. I remember because I waited for the shift change, and I remember looking at my watch when I got to the courthouse."

Driving to the Alderpoint area was different from driving to Redwood Point, but I saw no reason to bring that up.

"No further questions."

I stood. "Mr. Craw, was there any traffic delay when you drove up today?"

"No, sir."

"Thank you. I would like to excuse this witness and call Mr. William Thomas."

William Thomas had been part of my own avalanching. He lived near Aksana, but that had nothing to do with my reason for calling him. My misdirection—okay, my lie—had apparently worked because Bella's questioning of other witnesses suggested she didn't know about the bomb I was about to explode.

"Mr. Thomas," I began, "what is your profession?"

"I'm a truck driver. I drive a big rig between San Francisco and Crescent City. Also to small towns in between." Mr. Thomas looked like a truck driver and wore a Hard Rock Cafe t-shirt, black suspenders, and an odor of cigar.

"Can you tell me what happened in the early morning hours of August one?"

He fluttered his lips, sounding like a horse. "I wish I could forget. I jackknifed my truck."

"I'm sorry to hear that. Were you injured?"

"No, I was good."

"Where did this happen?"

"In the worst place of all." He looked down, possibly reliving the accident. "Richardson Grove."

A ripple went through the onlookers—Richardson Grove was famous. Various forces had been petitioning Caltrans to widen the road through the redwoods of Richardson Grove so larger trucks could serve the North Coast. Environmentalists objected because it would damage some old-growth trees. After years of protests and court hearings, the protestors won. The narrow road remained a bottleneck. If you drove from San Francisco to Redwood Point, you had to go through Richardson Grove.

"And what time did this happen?"

"It was around one thirty in the morning. The truck was wedged between two redwoods. It took CHP thirty minutes to arrive. The road was one hundred percent blocked."

"I see," I said. "What time did they clear the accident?"

"Not until four. My rig was wedged in good."

"Is there any other way to get from Petaluma to Alderpoint?"

"None that wouldn't take hours longer. You'd have to go inland from Longvale, take one sixty-eight to Route five, then take Route thirty-six from Red Bluff."

"How long would that take?"

He shook his head. "Ah, Christ—"

Bella stood. "Objection!"

"I'm sorry, judge," the trucker said, "I didn't mean to cuss."

Stevens looked confused for a second, like someone in my dad's wing of the nursing home, but she recovered. "No, not you, Mr. Thomas. Ms. Rivera?"

"May I approach?"

She gave permission, and we moved to the bench.

Bella gestured to Mr. Thomas. "This witness is not an expert on roadway travel times, Your Honor."

"On the contrary," I said, "he's been traveling this route for over ten years. What better expert could there be?"

"Judge," Bella said through gritted teeth, "Mr. Goodlove could have called a representative of Caltrans to the stand to testify about this accident. He called this witness instead, so as to obfuscate the reason for the testimony. To hide the existence of the accident on that night."

"Is that true, Mr. Goodlove?"

"Absolutely true."

Judge Stevens turned to the stenographer. "Could you give us a read-back from our sidebar during Ms. Cannon's testimony, starting with 'that's Mr. Goodlove's problem'?"

After a pause, the stenographer said, "Ms. Rivera: That's Mr. Goodlove's problem. He apparently doesn't know how to interview an opposing witness. Do I need to hold his hand or something?"

"Thank you, Maria. Ms. Rivera, I'm going to overrule the objection."

When I was back at the lectern, the truck driver asked me to repeat the question.

"How long would it have taken someone to detour around the accident in Richardson Grove?"

"At least nine hours."

"And you've been trucking in this area of California for how long?"

"Twelve years."

"No further questions."

Bella wisely decided not to cross-examine.

We were done for the day. I put some files into my briefcase while trying to grab that tip-of-my-brain thought. Something about the video. I replayed it in my head. When I was walking out the courtroom doors, it hit me like a truck. I froze, and someone bumped into me from behind.

Bingo.

Chapter Twenty-Two

JEN AND I RUSHED down to Detective Sergeant Granville's office. She was out, but we learned she'd be back in a few minutes. I waited in the echoey hallway, leaning back against the wall. Jen stood in front of me, tapping her foot.

"You going to tell me or not, boss?" Jen crossed her arms.

"Fingerprints."

"What about them?"

"When Aksana stretched her arm up at the Burger Pit, she might have touched the wall. She might have left a fingerprint. That would be just as good as seeing her face in the video."

"No, it's a long shot. They've probably washed the wall in the three months since then."

"Did cleanliness seem to be a high priority at the Burger Pit?" Even in the video, it looked like the place deserved a visit from the health department.

"No."

"That spot is high on the wall. No one cleans up that high. And fingerprints can last for decades." I once defended a guy whose fingerprints were found on a bottle of mulled wine in a house that had been burgled. Louella found that the mulled wine had been given to the homeowner by someone who had received it from my client. It had sat in the cupboard for twelve years, yet the fingerprints were as good as new.

Granville came down the hallway. Sometimes I thought she didn't really need the cane, that it was simply some kind of prop.

"Whom do we have here?" She looked from me to Jen. "May I presume that Miss Shek is here to report sexual harassment in the workplace? Ah, I do believe you are blushing, Mr. Goodlove."

We followed her into her office, and I wasted no time explaining my theory and requesting a fingerprint technician.

Granville thought for a while then said, "Do you share your partner's optimism, Ms. Shek?"

"Absolutely. It's worth pursuing." Jen was still skeptical, but she understood the importance of presenting a united front.

"I'm sorry, but I'm sure it would be impossible to get our fingerprint expert to go on what would be an all-night junket, something that in all likelihood would be for naught. Perhaps you could ask for a continuance." As she spoke, she worked away at her computer. Then she picked up her telephone, punched some buttons, and waited. "Ah, Frances. Would you be interested in going on a road trip?"

* * *

Frances turned out to be a tomboyish woman around fifty. I followed her into her cruiser, where she moved her seat forward so she could reach the pedals. I figured we'd get to the world-famous Burger Pit around eleven. I'd called to set things up and told them not to wash the wall. That request met with puzzled silence. Jen stayed in Redwood Point to keep the home fires burning. Or to sleep.

"Don't ask me to turn on the siren," Frances said.

I held my hands up in surrender. "Wouldn't think of it." How did she know I'd been thinking about how much time we could cut off the trip with the flashers on? "We can share driving if you want."

"Ha! I see. Someone wanted to be a policeman when he grew up. Do you want to play with my gun, too?" She had a smile on her face. And maybe a little leer?

I put on my seat belt. "Mind if I take a little nap, then?"

"I'll need you to navigate."

"Seriously?" It was a straight shot down 101 to Petaluma.

"And to keep me awake. You're lucky you're allowed to ride along at all. Granville must like you."

Frances enjoyed talking, and very little input on my end was needed to keep her awake. It turned out *she* had always wanted to be a cop when she was growing up—specifically, a fingerprint technician. She'd worked with the FBI for a spell, but had semiretired to Redwood Point because she liked its unhurried pace. We ended up using the light bar to bypass a horrific traffic jam in Santa Rosa and arrived at the burger joint at 11:10.

We borrowed a stepladder that allowed Frances to reach high enough up on the wall. The dusting didn't take long. She gave me a little lecture as she worked. "Latent fingerprints are made of three things. Sweat, oil, and protein. It's the oil that the magnetic fibers in the fingerprint powder cling to."

Interesting, but I didn't care. I only wanted to know whether Aksana's fingerprint was there.

She got two fingerprints from the wall, transferring them with special tape to something she called a "lift card." We went back to the patrol car to make the comparison. I had trouble breathing, maybe because I was holding my breath.

Frances put on a magnifying headset and looked back and forth between the first print and Aksana's. "That's a no-go on this one."

She compared the second one with Aksana's and froze. "That's odd. Weird!"

"What?"

"This … this print isn't human. It's from a monkey." She turned to me. "An orangutan, actually."

"What!?"

She laughed and punched me on the thigh. "Just kidding. It matches. Aksana, you *are* the father." She laughed more. "Man, you should have seen your face."

In chambers the next morning, Bella almost blew out a heart valve trying to keep the new fingerprint evidence from being admitted. Frances wasn't enough of an expert, the prosecution hadn't been given enough notice, they would have to demand a continuance, it was trial by ambush, and several other desperate arguments. She was breathing hard.

I said, "Your Honor, the only delay was caused by the prosecution not doing its job. They were so intent on convicting my client they ignored this exculpatory evidence, failing to do the obvious thing and collect the fingerprints long ago."

Bella stood over me. "If it was so obvious, why didn't you think of it? Sooner."

"Their zeal to convict," I said, "even makes me wonder whether …"

Everyone waited.

"No. Sorry. Nothing." I'd been about to accuse Bella of planting the blood and hair evidence, but I didn't believe that, and doing so would be going too far. Plus, Bella would have strangled me right there in chambers.

"Let me think about this." Judge Stevens closed her eyes and kept them closed so long that I was sure she'd decided to sleep on it.

Finally she blinked them open but said nothing.

Jen spoke up for the first time in the meeting. "Your Honor, Ms. Rivera's arguments that we couldn't be confident it was Aksana in the video were cogent and compelling. She suggested the video isn't sufficient evidence of her alibi. The fingerprints tell us our client was indeed at the restaurant. They are crucial."

Stevens took a deep breath. "How much more do you have, Mr. Goodlove?"

"If you allow the fingerprints, I'll have RPPD's fingerprint expert testify, then I'll present the credit card data, examine an employee of the Burger Pit who remembers seeing Aksana, and that will be it."

"Okay," she said, "I will allow the fingerprint evidence."

Louella was sure that if Aksana were some kind of professional criminal, she would have run afoul of a police department somewhere in the country. She had never been arrested, since her fingerprints weren't in the system, but that didn't necessarily mean she had escaped attention.

Unfortunately, Louella no longer had the clout that came from announcing she was with LAPD robbery-homicide. *That had always opened doors and loosened tongues.* When she called veteran detectives in police departments around the country, she found that most were tired of private eyes. However, she could usually get jaded cops interested in the story of a hit woman who looked like an aging babushka. She'd already talked to the police in many cities with no hits, but Garrett wanted her to keep going. The trial was almost over, but he still wanted her to look into Aksana's background. *Does he just want to satisfy his curiosity?*

During her dinner with Aksana, talk had turned to unusual buildings, and Ms. Ivanova had mentioned a gas station in the shape of a shell. Through a Google search, Louella found the landmark in Winston-Salem, North Carolina, so she'd called their police department. Detective Nelson Fagan had neglected to return several calls, but she finally got him on the line.

"Fagan."

Louella smiled. Even with that one word, his Southern accent came through.

"Detective Fagan, this is Louella Davis calling from California. I used to be with the LAPD, but I've moved up to a small town in Northern California, and I'm working on an interesting homicide case here."

He spoke with someone in the background then said, "I'm listening."

"This is an older woman, age seventy, who is accused of killing someone with a submachine pistol. It's an unusual case because the woman looks like a grandmother, not a killer."

The line was silent.

"Detective Fagan, are you still there?"

"Is she overweight, with a head scarf?"

Chills ran down Louella's spine. "Yes."

"Looks like one of them babushka ladies?"

"Detective, I think we're talking about the same woman."

"I've been waiting for this call. Hold on." He yelled out to someone, "Harry, pick up line three. The babushka." Into the phone, he repeated, "I've been waiting for this call. Tell me who you are again and where you're calling from."

Louella filled him in on the details of the case. "There's another murder that may be connected. A sniper-style killing with an exploding bullet."

"Well, I'll tell y'all what we had here a few years ago. There was a trial here, one of those class …"

"Class actions," another voice said.

"Yeah, class action. That's one of my associates on the line. So anyway, this was a big deal trial about fraud in the tobacco company, Thompson-Sutter. You know them, right?"

"Of course." They were the world's second largest tobacco producer.

"Yeah, so anyway, it was security fraud."

"Securities." Harry's voice was lower, and he had a slight lisp.

"Yeah, whatever. So, there were two accountants who'd turned state's evidence, and they were going to testify against Thompson-Sutter. One week before the trial, one of them is killed right in front of our officers. He was in a hotel room, and he got too close to a window. An hour later, the other one was found dead. He'd refused protection and had gone out backpacking, not telling anyone where he'd gone. He was a survivalist and thought he could protect himself. Anyway, some hikers heard a burst of gunfire and said it sounded like a machine gun. They'd seen an older woman a little earlier. They remembered her because she didn't look like your typical backpacker. They said she was really old and looked like a farm woman from Russia. She'd been smiley and had an accent."

Harry added, "One of the backpacking witnesses was an artist, and he drew a sketch of her. From memory. Really good. We'll send it to you. Three other people reported seeing her in town. One sighting was near the hotel where the witness was shot. They looked at the sketch and were like, 'Wow, yeah. That's her!' Overweight, head scarf, big smile. About the last person you'd suspect of being a paid killer."

"Yeah," Fagan said. "We got no physical evidence, no fingerprints, and no one ever spotted her again. We figure she left right after the executions. That's what I call them, executions, 'cause that's what they were. We uploaded what we had to the NCIC database, but we never had a hit. Wait, you said you're private?"

"That's right."

"So how did you find us?"

Louella explained, gave Fagan her email address, and the Winston-Salem detectives forwarded her everything they had. It wasn't much, but the sketch sent more chills down her spine.

Louella checked her watch. *Garrett will be giving closing statements about now.* She headed to the courthouse.

Chapter Twenty-Three

AFTER WE'D DOTTED OUR i's, crossed our t's, and rested our case, Bella stood for her closing argument. I didn't envy her. Jen and I had heaped reasonable doubt onto all her evidence showing Aksana had been at the scene of the crime. She'd been unable to shoot down the fingerprint evidence. She did a masterful job, however, and didn't resort to any underhanded tactics.

Bella made our theory of the planted hair and blood evidence seem contrived. Would someone really go to all that trouble? Why hadn't they just killed her? She pooh-poohed the idea that someone else with Aksana's tires had driven close to Shipley's farm. Of course the witness noticed Aksana's sports car, a vehicle that was totally out of place on those washboard roads. The bundle of cash demonstrated that the defendant was a criminal, and the fact it was gone soon after she paid her bond further cemented her guilt in this particular crime.

She supported her arguments with replays of portions of the videotaped testimony. That was inspired, and I resolved to do the same in the future. She played back only those snippets she wanted the jury to hear and argued as to why they were so important. For example, she played a clip in which the eyewitness said, "I know what I saw, and I saw that sports car." She didn't bore the jurors by summarizing testimony, she didn't attack Jen or me, and she didn't overstate the evidence.

She sat. My turn.

I whispered in Jen's ear. "I think you should do it."

"What? You want me to do the closing argument?"

I nodded.

"That's crazy, Garrett. You've prepared it. It's your forte. What—why?"

Judge Stevens' voice cut into their discussion. "Mr. Goodlove?"

"I'm sorry, Your Honor. Just another few seconds, please."

The judge assented, and I told Jen, "I'm not convinced of Aksana's innocence, and I worry that the jurors will see that."

Jen swore in Chinese. Or Japanese. Maybe both. "That's ridiculous. You've closed many times for a client you knew was guilty. Later we can have a lecture about how the legal system works in this country. The same one you've given me in the past. Now man up and do your job."

She was right, as usual. I took a deep breath, adjusted my attitude, and stood.

"Ladies and gentlemen of the jury, as the prosecutor said in her opening statement, you guys lucked out. Her case is so weak that you'll have no trouble reaching a verdict. We've shown you a video of Aksana hours away from Mr. Shipley's farm when the murder occurred. Sure, we couldn't see her face, but we have something better: her fingerprint. You had the opportunity to actually see the finger pressed against the wall. How often does that happen? RPPD's own expert testified that the fingerprint was left by Aksana. The prosecution hasn't denied that."

I hit the high points, emphasized the problems with Bella's evidence, and then put a map of Northern California on an easel. "When you're deliberating, I want you to picture this map. It all boils down to this: If she was here—" I tapped the tip of the pointer against Petaluma, the location of the Burger Pit "—she couldn't have been in Alderpoint." I tapped Alderpoint.

I let that sink in for a moment, then I repeated it, using more force with the pointer. "If she was here—" *Whap!* "—she couldn't have been here." *Whap!* Like Johnny Cochran's "If it doesn't fit, you must acquit" but with better sound effects.

I sat down. Aksana nodded and squeezed my arm.

Jen smiled. "That's the old Garrett I know and love," she said.

Jen and I stared at the sketch Louella had shared with us. Calling it a sketch didn't do it justice. The artist was a master of photorealism, and I had to look closely to determine that it wasn't a black-and-white photograph. There was no denying that the woman in the drawing was our client.

I looked at my watch. "Aksana will be here any minute."

Jen frowned. "Here? Why?"

"I want to prepare her for the verdict."

"You've done that already."

"It can't hurt." I slid the sketch into a drawer in my desk.

At that moment, Aksana knocked and waddled in, dropping into her usual place on the couch. "Oy!" She stood again, rubbed her butt, and laughed. "Is something here."

How can she seem so unconcerned? The length of the deliberations suggested the jurors did not see things as slam-dunk obvious.

"Oh, sorry, Aksana. You can put that on my desk." I'd finally found the perfect doorknob for my man cave, and I'd absentmindedly left it on the couch. I made a mental note to clear a space in a drawer for my hardware instead of leaving it around. Unprofessional.

Watching her, I still had trouble picturing her as a for-hire killer.

The phone rang.

I listened and put down the receiver. "The jury's back."

On the drive to the courthouse, I prepped Aksana for the trauma of hearing the verdict. We went in and took our seats at the defense table.

Most people experience only a handful of times when their future is revealed in a dramatic moment. Opening the letter from college admissions, for example, getting the call from the doctor on your lab results, or finding out whether you're pregnant. Hearing a verdict when you're on trial for murder is off-the-charts stressful.

The jury filed into the courtroom. Aksana grabbed my hand and clutched it until all the blood seemed to be squeezed out of it. I never liked the wait as the formalities were run through. It would have been better if the first juror through the door just yelled, "Guilty!" or "Not Guilty!"

Finally, Judge Stevens addressed the foreperson. "Have you reached a verdict?"

"We have not, Your Honor."

Not! Everyone in the courtroom gasped. It was a hung jury.

The judge polled the jurors, confirming that each one felt there was absolutely no chance of coming to a consensus. She did not insist that they continue deliberating. Before Stevens could thank and excuse the jurors, Inspector Granville came into the courtroom and up the aisle. Everyone seemed to realize that something important was about to happen. Granville received permission to enter the well, went up to Judge Stevens, and conferred with her. She handed Stevens a sheet of paper. Granville left without looking at me or anyone else.

Stevens finished excusing the jurors and asked counsel to join her in chambers. I looked over at Bella, and she shrugged. She seemed genuinely baffled, so it wasn't one of her tricks. We followed the judge as she doddered back to her desk.

When we had all settled in, she took a deep breath. "It seems, ladies and gentleman, that someone has confessed to the murder of Mr. Dean Shipley."

The three of us sat, turned to stone.

Jen recovered first. "Who?"

Stevens looked at the paper Granville had handed her. "A Mr. Peter Barks."

Sleepy Pete!

"He turned himself in?" I asked.

Stevens shook her head. "He turned himself in to a higher authority."

"Higher authority?"

"He committed suicide. He passed a hose from the exhaust pipe of his car into the passenger compartment. Before he died, he penned a suicide note via text. I'll read it to you."

The judge held the paper in front of her and cleared her throat several times. "A gang paid me to shot Dean and they took away his body. Also, he didn't respect the land that I fawt for. I threw my gun away on one-oh-one." She looked up. "He spelled 'fought' f-a-w-t."

"And *shot* instead of *shoot*?" I asked.

"Yes."

Following the mistrial, the prosecution could choose to dismiss the charges or retry the case. The suicide note would be catastrophic unless it could be proven to be fabricated. In any event, it would introduce considerable doubt.

Stevens cleared her throat again. "Ms. Rivera, do you wish to dismiss the charges against Aksana Ivanova?"

If the charges were dismissed, Aksana could not be retried. Double jeopardy rules attach as soon as testimony is heard. Our client would be free, her nightmare ended.

Bella looked down at the floor, chewing on her lip. Then she looked over at me. I looked her in the eyes and made a movement that could have gotten me disbarred.

With our gazes locked, I rotated my head about a millimeter to the left and then back again. An almost imperceptible shake of the head. *Did she get the message?*

Bella said. "Not at this time, Your Honor."

Chapter Twenty-Four

WE HELD THE WRAP party at Carly's. Normally, Aksana would have been invited, but I didn't want to have anything more to do with her. I kept things cordial when I told her I wouldn't be handling her retrial if there was one. I was tempted to make some excuse—say I'd be busy with some other trial—but I told her only that I couldn't do it. Maybe that was a mistake—I didn't want to be on her bad side.

Zach, Carly's muscle-tough bodyguard, met me at her door. His services had no longer been required once the nine-fingered man had been blown away. Maybe I should have been surprised to see him, but I wasn't.

"Ah, the baby brother," he signed with a wink.

I laughed and signed back, "How is it you haven't been scared off yet? She must be hiding her true self."

He put his right hand on the back of his left and drew it toward his elbow: "Slow down."

I gave him a hearty handshake and repeated my joke out loud.

"ASL only, remember?" he signed, looking around with mock fear as if worried about a hiding mountain lion. "Or Carly will whip my butt."

I hoped that Carly would keep him around for a long time.

Toby came over and showed me some photos from his "backpacking" trip. He'd hiked not the forest or the mountains, but the wilds of San Francisco. Living rough on the streets, he'd documented the experience with photos for a story on homelessness. Not smart, but very Toby.

Carly poked my side, and when I turned she signed, "All hail the conquering hero."

"More like a draw," I said.

"I heard it was ten to two for acquittal."

"Who told you that?"

She pointed toward the deck, where Louella was talking with Jen.

She winked. "Do you like Zach?"

I snapped my fingers. "I forgot to tell you. He's your early Christmas present from Nicole and me, so don't go expecting anything else."

She laughed and gave me a hug. I hadn't seen her that happy in years. I was hoping the party would give me some relief from my unease about the outcome of the trial, and the hug indeed helped.

Wishing that Nicole—away at law school—could be there, too, I went out to the deck, where Louella was making her contribution to the late afternoon fog. I pulled a beer from the cooler and sat next to my partner. Jen put her hand on my arm.

"So," Louella said, "you didn't buy the suicide, did you?"

I kept my voice low. "Not for a second."

"Right. Granville told me Pete's fingerprints weren't where they should have been on the hose or the duct tape. They found a trace of some drugs in his system that aren't of your regular recreational variety."

I nodded. "So, our babushka, having heard about Pete's hobby, waits until he's passed out in his car, gives him some additional drug to make sure he won't wake up, rigs up the hose, writes the suicide note, and turns on the engine."

"Something like that." She blew out a fruity-smelling cloud. "I assume Aksana knew about his routine?"

"Yeah. We'd talked about it in front of her at some point. His phone wasn't password or fingerprint protected?"

"It was not." Louella sucked in another drag.

"So, one bad, two good," I said.

Jen frowned. "What do you mean?"

"Aksana killed one bad guy, the guy who kidnapped me and who deserved to die, and two good, honest people, Dean Shipley and Sleepy Pete."

Louella sighed. "Plus two good guys in North Carolina."

I wondered about how many other innocents she'd executed. "Anything on the jury tampering?"

"*Possible* jury tampering," Louella said. "I mentioned it to Granville, but she agreed there wasn't enough there to investigate further. All I can say is it's a good thing they didn't acquit."

An acquittal would have meant she could never be retried.

"Doesn't matter," Jen said. "They'll never try her again anyway without new evidence. We discredited everything they have."

"I'm going to have a hard time living with that," I said.

If what Louella told me about the other crimes was right, then I was looking at five murders by my client, Aksana. My ex-client. I'd washed my hands of her, and hopefully I'd never see her again. But I couldn't get over the logic that undoubtedly had swayed most of the jury members. If Aksana was at the Burger Pit at 2:00 a.m., she simply could not have been on Shipley's farm when he was shot. Maybe Bella was right and he'd been killed outside of that time window, but my arguments against that had been compelling.

Two days after the wrap party, I sat in my office, a fire crackling in the fireplace and seagulls crying outside. I brought up the video again. I ran it up to the moment Aksana put her hand against the wall. The movement looked even more ridiculous than before. *What kind of crazy-ass stretch is that?*

I paused it when her hand touched the wall and stared. I zoomed in. Was the shadow wrong? Still zoomed in, I moved the video forward and back, frame by frame. I froze. I did it again. Her hand didn't actually touch the wall. But I knew her fingerprint was there, so it must have. Right?

Damn! The pieces clunked into place. *What a conniving liar she is, but can I confirm it?*

The Burger Pit owner had provided a full two weeks of video, one week on each side of the night of the murder. I started with the very first recording and fast-forwarded at high speed. I was sure I wouldn't miss it.

There! Four days before the murder, someone came in and went through the same ridiculous stretch. Aksana. The real Aksana. This time she pressed an index finger firmly and deliberately against the wall. She was planting evidence. She must have had someone else come in at the time she planned to kill Shipley. Someone with a similar body. Like a sister. An accessory before the fact. The fingerprint was there, and the video fooled us into thinking it had been made at the time of the murder. It was a good assumption. One that Aksana had depended on.

I nodded. Now all the fast-food bags in her car—despite the neatness of her house—made sense. If there had been only one, and if she'd brought up the alibi, we might have been more suspicious. Instead, she let us think it was our idea to check receipt times.

Finding the place in the dark was tricky, and it took me longer than I'd planned. The sun would be up soon. I turned off the rented truck's engine. Automatic weapons fire sounded in the distance. *What was that all about?* I didn't want to know.

My heart banging against my ribcage, I put on the headlamp I'd bought for this mission and picked up my toolbox from the passenger seat. The skunk-like odor of marijuana was everywhere. Or maybe it was a real skunk. The wind rustled the leaves of the alder trees, and something metal creaked. Maybe a rusty sign.

Last chance to turn back. This was perhaps the worst thing I'd ever done. *No. It is the correct thing to do.* When I was seven, I'd decided I would jump off the high board at the pool. I figured it wouldn't kill me, so I vowed to ignore my fear. I resolved that once I started up that ladder, I wouldn't turn back. No matter what. I was terrified, but I jumped.

This was the same. I'd resolved to do it, and I would.

With gloved hands, I found an unlatched window and slid it up. I levered myself over the sill and started to fall, not knowing what I'd land on. But, with my hands and waist on the sill, I tipped over until my face smashed into the unfinished plywood wall below the window, knocking off my headlamp. I must have looked ridiculous.

The headlamp, now on the dirt floor, showed me there was nothing sharp to fall on, so I let myself drop, twisting and landing on my side. *I'll be sore tomorrow.* I straightened out, put the headlamp back on, and went to the door to the outside. I opened it, got my toolbox, and went back in.

There. The closet I remembered. *This will work.* The job was tricky given my limited handyman skills and the special demands of the situation. It went well, however. When I finished, I closed the window, put my tools away, counted them twice, as a surgeon counts the sponges he uses, and left.

Louella sat in her living room reading the *Times Standard*, her feet up on an ottoman. When she saw the article about Aksana, she put down her tea. *Well, I didn't expect that.*

Yesterday, bail was revoked for Ms. Aksana Ivanova three weeks after her murder trial ended in a mistrial. According to a source with knowledge of the investigation, the police received an anonymous tip suggesting they recheck for fingerprints in a shed on the property of the deceased, Dean Shipley.

According to the source, fingerprints on a glass doorknob place Ms. Ivanova at the scene of the murder. In addition, the tipster provided information that cast doubt on Ivanova's visit to a Burger Pit that had provided her with an alibi. Finally, a new search of her house uncovered a secret hiding place containing several passports under different names, all with Ms. Ivanova's photograph.

Because the death of Peter Barks was ruled a homicide, his supposed suicide note will not be a factor in the next trial. The date for a new trial has not yet been announced.

She picked up her tea and sipped it. *Who has a glass doorknob in a shed?*

Chapter Twenty-Five

I STOOD OUTSIDE THE door taking deep breaths. I hadn't expected my violation of the principles of my profession to weigh so heavily on my mind. It had seemed like the right thing to do. The socially responsible thing to do. Plant the evidence like a dirty cop and make sure that The Babushka never murdered another soul. On a practical level, keeping the information to myself was the only way to retain my license to practice law. So I'd planned to take the secret to my grave, not revealing it even to Jen. But it had eaten away at my soul. I couldn't hold it inside.

Confession time. Squaring my shoulders, I knocked, opened the door, and walked in.

I took a deep breath and announced, "I did a terrible thing."

My father blinked a few times and turned to me. Some days he didn't know who I was. Would this be one of those days?

"Gary, you're such a good boy. I'm sure you're blowing it out of proportion. Tell me what happened."

I took a balled-up napkin from his food tray and wiped the drool from the corner of his mouth. The tray held something that looked like baby food and smelled like liver.

"I planted evidence. That's the worst kind of crime."

"Why didn't you tell me, son? I could have helped you with that."

He'd always liked stories, so I recounted my adventure, describing in particular how it had taken all my home improvement skills to install the doorknob—the one I'd placed on the couch just before Aksana had come to my office—without smudging her prints or adding my own. I explained how I'd had more than sufficient evidence that she was the international hit woman known as The Babushka.

Dad put his hand on my head. "Gary, you did the right thing. The other kids on the bus never liked her."

I smiled and blinked back some tears, not for my actions but for the time that had been stolen from my father. At least he was happy in his ignorance. Hopefully, that would be me someday.

Perhaps I'd soon despise myself again, but at that moment I saw things clearly: I'd told a terrible lie, but it was a lie worth telling.

Aksana sat alone in her jail cell, regretting her mistakes. She shouldn't have taken a contract so close to her new hideaway, but it was such a simple job. Shoot a man in the woods. Who knew why the tobacco company wanted it done? Who cared? The other contractors did the rest—they got rid of the body. They were pros, and she didn't fault them. Not in a million years would anyone imagine that a shark would provide the police with the bullet. *Still seems impossible.*

She stood and wrapped her hands around the bars of her cell.

Keeping the gun—that was her biggest mistake. It had been given to her by her uncle and mentor, Jaroslav. The master. She had planned to throw it away, but when the time came she couldn't do it. *Ya stareyu. I am getting too old.*

And she should have fled as soon as she made bail. She missed two opportunities to do that. She could have found a new hideaway as good as the one in Humboldt.

She smiled. Killing the lawyer's kidnapper had felt like good old days. *Bang, boom.* Her contact had identified him and ordered the hit. The local, amateurish gang of growers had been causing too much trouble.

Killing the Vietnam soldier? *Prosto. Simple.* He was already half gone, drugged up in his old car. Give him a little booster shot, write the suicide note, feed exhaust into the car's cabin, turn on the engine, go. *Prosto.*

She laughed when she thought about defeating the old-style ankle monitor. It would have reported a lack of movement. Was funny to think of it wandering around her house, duct taped to her Roomba while she was getting away with murder. Twice.

The soldier was her eleventh. Or was she losing count?

The fingerprints at the hamburger place to create a just-in-case alibi, that had been a nice touch. Her sister from Redding had gone in at the perfect time. And burying the receipt in among all the garbage in her car

—that was why no one thought it was planted there intentionally. *Am genius.*

But her fingerprints on the doorknob? *Impossible. Didn't go in the shed. How could someone plant my fingerprints?*

Da, ya stareyu. Yes, I'm getting too old.

Jen opened the door to her home. She was stunning in her LBD. It was the same one she'd worn when we'd snuggled the night away on my couch. If she was trying to lift me out of my funk, it was working.

She'd made a delicious meal of Hungarian goulash with home-baked French bread. Quite a difference from the meals of her parents' homelands, but it worked. The scent of onions, garlic, and paprika hung in the air.

After dinner she joined me on the couch holding something behind her back, a smile tugging at the corners of her mouth.

I looked at her sideways. "You hiding something, counselor?"

"Maybe."

I reached behind her, but she twisted away.

"Let me explain," she said then leaned forward and kissed me. I moved toward her for more, but she held up a hand. "I was thinking, Garrett, that—"

"Are you blushing?"

"Hush," she said. "I was thinking that because marijuana was such a large part of this case, and because we live in the Emerald Triangle, and much of our work in the future might relate to it, that …"

"That what?"

She pulled a chocolate bar out from behind her back.

"What? We should eat chocolate?"

She smiled. "This isn't chocolate. I mean it isn't *just* chocolate."

That was a surprise. "Huh."

"It's marijuana chocolate. An edible. I've done some research and determined that we should eat only one square each. It's legal. What do you think, boss?"

"Hold on, Jen. I'm all for it, but I want to be very clear about something."

"Well?"

I took a breath. "I'm not sure if you know this, but marijuana usually makes one very …"

She cocked her head. "What? Very what?"

"Affectionate … and horny."

She gave me her inscrutable look and popped two squares into her mouth.

Acknowledgments

I'm so grateful for the help I've had with this book.

I had an insightful beta-reader crew, as usual. Thanks to my wonderful wife, Lena, who is always the first reader for my books. Special thanks to Navtej Nandra, Linda Johnson, Gail Summerville, Diane Orton, Bruce Lutz, Wisteria, Wendy J. Porter, Becky Jolly, Rex Last, and others.

My copy editor, Julie MacKenzie from FreeRangeEditorial.com, always does a wonderful job. I may need to tone down my praise of her, because the more clients she picks up, the less time she'll have for editing my books!

Also by Al Macy

Becoming a Great Sight-Reader—or Not! Learn from my Quest for Piano Sight-Reading Nirvana
Drive, Ride, Repeat: The Mostly True Account of a Cross-Country Car and Bicycle Adventure

Contact Us: A Jake Corby Sci-Fi Thriller
The Antiterrorist: A Jake Corby Sci-Fi Thriller
The Universe Next Door: A Jake Corby Sci-Fi Thriller
The Christmas Planet and Other Stories

Yesterday's Thief: An Eric Beckman Paranormal Sci-Fi Thriller
Sanity's Thief: An Eric Beckman Paranormal Thriller
Democracy's Thief: An Eric Beckman Paranormal Thriller
A Mind Reader's Christmas: An Eric Beckman Mystery
The Day Before Yesterday's Thief: A Prequel to the Eric Beckman Series
Yesterday's Thief, Tomorrow's Science

The Protected Witness: An Alex Booker Thriller
The Abducted Heiress: An Alex Booker Thriller
* * *

Al Macy

Conclusive Evidence: A Novel

About the Author

Al Macy lives with his wife on the far reaches of the North Coast of California, on the outskirts of a town with only four hundred residents. The settings for his Goodlove and Shek legal thrillers come not from his imagination but from his everyday world. While working at his rolltop desk, he's fortunate enough to be able to look out at the spruce, pine, and redwood forest that surrounds his house.

During his working life, Macy was a neuroscientist, educational computer game programmer, jazz trombonist, jazz pianist, cook, CEO, clam digger, and technical writer. He now devotes most of his time to writing stories.

Made in the USA
Middletown, DE
02 December 2020